I0544732

Triple Diamond

WILD FLOWERS

GEMMA SNOW

Wild Flowers
ISBN # 978-1-913186-18-0
©Copyright Gemma Snow 2018
Cover Art by Posh Gosh ©Copyright September 2018
Interior text design by Claire Siemaszkiewicz
Totally Bound Publishing

Published in 2019 by Totally Bound Publishing, United Kingdom.

Totally Bound Publishing is an imprint of Totally Entwined Group Limited.

WILD FLOWERS

Dedication

To Robbie, my very own Mountain Man.

My family, always.

Rebecca, for making it happen, time and again.

Prologue

Lily pulled the bottle from the drawer but didn't open it. In the stark light from the flower refrigerator behind her, the golden whiskey cast a long shadow across her desk. She stared out of the front window of A Rose By Any Other Name, imagining the downtown San Francisco scene outside. The fridge kept up its low buzz, but she could still hear the city. A million people she couldn't see, riding on bicycles and in cars and trolleys, people with someplace to go, someplace to be, someone to meet. She lived in one of America's favorite cities, filled to the brim with bustle and hustle, and still she found some way to feel so incredibly, remarkably alone.

She gritted her teeth. Fuck alone. *Fuck* alone. Five years and she'd been damn well getting over these lingering, shadowed moments of self-pity and desperate thinking. She'd had half a decade to compartmentalize and manage her emotions. Five years of being sad, whatever sort of insignificant word that was for the grief that had almost consumed her so very many times. Well, in truth, a hell of a lot longer than five years. The days sort of blended together after a while.

But, though time passed, the anniversary never got any easier, and with her sister and best friend Madison now living all the way out on a ranch in Montana she'd inherited from an uncle she'd never met, Lily felt more alone than ever.

Of course, she wasn't alone. She visited her parents, still living in the house where she'd grown up across the city, all the time. She had the shop, too, the shop she slaved over day in and day out—the same shop that, years after opening, she found herself questioning if it really was everything she wanted.

Between her and the cold roses and the unopened whiskey and the dark, she could admit that it wasn't. But, God, all those years ago, she'd promised Daniel, promised him something and stuck to it with every part of who she was. This shop was going to be theirs. It would be their baby—their lives. They would work together and raise a family together and live together until they were older than the dirt in which her African violets were grown.

But life had other plans and, now, well, a shop was a poor substitute for the man she had loved with her whole heart. In fact, she wasn't sure it was any sort of substitute anymore. And if she was asking that now, if she was no longer content to spend twelve-hour days slaving over wedding bouquets for other people's happily-ever-afters… Yes, if she was over the constant grind of just trying to stay afloat in the most expensive city in the entire freaking country, that meant it was time.

She pulled her laptop out of the desk cubby and opened her email service, tapping her fingers against her chin, waiting for the program to load. The whiskey was still unopened on the desk, which meant this wasn't some impulsive drunken decision. And it wasn't just the anniversary, either. No, this thought had been percolating in her head for a while, always coming back, no matter how many times she pushed it away. Which could only mean one thing. *You're ready, Lil. It really is time.*

Daniel would have said the same thing.

So she opened a new email, the screen so bright and white in the stark darkness of her closed shop, and she typed in an email address she had never thought she would write to again.

Dear Dr. Malachi,

You told me to be in touch when I felt the time had come to continue my work, no matter how long that took. At the time, I never believed returning to my research would feel like the right choice. I now understand that you knew more than I did what I needed in those dark days, and yes, in fact, I find that I am ready to complete my research, after all. I thank you for your patience and infinite wisdom and hope to see you in the near future.

All the best,

Lily Hollis

There. That was done. She shut her computer and allowed her eyes to adjust to the store's dim light once again. Christ on a calla lily, was it possible that one email could somehow make her feel capable of breathing all over again? She had to be imagining the enormity of the weight now lifted from her shoulders, a weight she had never even realized was there, but one she had walked around with for so many years.

She was…free?

And terrified. Completely and utterly terrified. And for that reason and so many more, she reached for the bottle of whiskey that she had pulled out on this night for the last five years and never opened, unscrewed the cap and took a long drink. She wasn't going to regret this decision and she wasn't going to overanalyze it. No, she was done living in the past. It was time to be part of her own life again and she was about to find out exactly what that meant.

Chapter One

"We've got a scent!"

Axel was trying hard not to get too far ahead of Micah to see, and Micah did his best to keep pace, following the large and very determined golden retriever down a steep incline, clenching his thighs and lowering his center of gravity to avoid sliding on the wet, fallen leaves that coated the Clark Mountain Range of Glacier National Park, at the edge of the Montana–Canada border. Axel, on his four legs, was doing a much better job holding his grip on the ground, but Micah had no desire to go sliding off the edge of the mountain and into the depths of the canyons below, so he whistled a command and the dog slowed enough for Micah to catch up.

Still, they kept an admirable pace and quickly came to a plateau of flat ground. High above, at the top of the ridge, Micah heard his partner Dec — Deckard McCormick — approaching with Rosie, Axel's sister. Rosie kicked up a pile of leaves on the approach, clearly picking up on the same scent Axel had.

"Anything down there?" Dec shouted, the sound catching and echoing off the many flat walls of the mountain range.

"I think I saw a cave," Micah called back, straining to look around the corner of a large boulder that jutted forth from the ground and mountainside. "Give me a second. I'll let you know whether or not to come down."

Dec gave the affirmative then Micah crouched low to peer around the edge of the boulder.

Oh, shit.

That wasn't just a boulder. That was the edge of the fucking mountain, looking down over a sheer two hundred foot drop to the canyon below. For a fleeting, horrible second, vertigo caught his senses and nearly dragged him to his knees, making the sky and the high trees waver and tilt.

But Micah put a steadying hand on the rock wall and took a deep breath, settling the sky firmly above him and the ground firmly below. He commanded Axel to stay put — not that he needed to. Axel was a damn smart dog and knew better than to go canyon jumping. Then Micah lay flat on his stomach, damn near hanging over the edge of the mountain, to look around the boulder's protruding side.

There was definitely a cave on the other side, a yawning, darkened mouth, gaping right over the valley. The question was — was there anyone in it?

"Hello," he called, his breath labored and caught, what with his stomach pressed against the ground. And he was still pressed against the ground. He had to keep reminding himself of that. The stones and wet leaves that rasped against his forearms, giving a slight fall chill in the mountains, were all real. For this moment, at least, he wasn't plummeting toward certain death below.

"Is there anyone in the cave?" *A pause.* The silence was weighty, colored by the sounds of raptors flying overhead and wind rippling through the trees that towered high above the ground, giving Micah a very odd sense of perspective as to exactly how far up in the sky he was.

Oh, about ten thousand feet…

But now was just about the worst time to calculate the distance it would take to kill a grown man, so he focused his attention on the solid ground and his mission and called out again. "This is Lewis and Clark County Search and Rescue Agent Micah Ellison, I repeat, is there anyone in the cave?"

A sound. It was barely even a real sound and if he hadn't been trained by the very best to determine the difference between human and nature, he might not have heard it. But there it was, a whimper catching on the wind, the softest, shuddering inhalation of a very terrified child.

Chloe Robinson. Female. African American. Six years old and approximately thirty-nine inches tall. Last seen Tuesday, October Eight. Amber alert issued Wednesday, October Nine.

She'd been gone a week. In the world of search and rescue, a week was no better than a month was no better than a year. It was true what they said about forty-eight hours. Truer still when the Montana mountain ranges, of which there were many, were known for being unforgiving and merciless. Micah knew all about that first-hand.

But there was no denying the signs of life coming from the other side of the boulder. After nearly a decade of doing this job, Micah knew the sound of a frightened child all too well and unless the universe played some pretty hairy tricks, the girl on the other side of that sheer drop down to the valley was Chloe Robinson.

"Chloe," he called out, hoping the sound would carry and not get lost on the wind, as any calls he made toward Dec and the team undoubtedly would. "Chloe Robinson."

The sound of her fearful whimpering increased and when he called her name again, this time she answered him. *Thank fuck for small victories.*

"How do you know my name?"

But that was the way of kids, wasn't it? Find them hidden in a darkened cave in the middle of a mountain range and they want to know how you know their name.

"Your mom and dad told me," Micah replied. "See, they've been missing you and they sent me and my partner Dec out to see if we could find you with our dogs, Axel and Rosie. Do you like dogs, Chloe?"

A small sniff echoed across the gap, then, "I have a dog…at home. Her name is Daisy."

Micah sighed in relief. Good, she was talking, which meant she wasn't too dehydrated to function or too badly injured. He hoped.

"Well, Chloe, I'd really like to get you back home to Daisy, okay?" he said. "Now, I'm going to talk to my partner, but I'll be right back…"

"No!" she shouted the word before he even finished his sentence. "Stay. Don't leave. I don't want to be alone anymore."

Micah nodded and as carefully as he could, reached for the radio on his utility belt.

"Okay, I'm not leaving," he said. "But I'm going to talk to him over the radio, okay? I just want to let him know that I found you, all right?"

She sniffled but agreed and Micah brought the radio to his mouth, doing his damnedest to think about Chloe, the brave as all hell six-year-old in the cave, and not the freaking mountainous drop right below his face.

"Dec," he radioed over. "She's here." The radio crackled in and out, then cut out completely, plunging the mountain's edge into silence that suddenly felt a whole hell of a lot colder and lonelier than it had a minute ago.

Or maybe that was just the clouds rolling in overhead. *For fuck's sake.*

Okay, okay. He'd dealt with hairier situations than this and he was damn well going to get that girl out of the cave if it was his last act on earth and all that. He sent up a prayer to as many of his gods as he could remember in the moment then called back to the little girl.

"Just you and me now, Chloe, okay?" he said. "Now, I'm going to hook my belaying chord to a tree on this side of the gap then I'm coming over to you. You can talk to me. I can hear you."

He stood and stepped a foot in from the edge of the cliff, allowing himself one deep breath before walking over to the thick oak tree growing sideways out of the mountain. He tested a branch with his weight, finding it thick and sturdy, before tossing the end of the rope around it and securing the knot that he had been tying since he was about Chloe's age. He tugged on the end attached to his security belt and, satisfied, returned to the edge of the mountain.

"How did you end up here, Chloe?" *Don't look down, Micah.*

"I got lost," Chloe said, only a slight sniffle to her voice. *Christ, this six-year-old little girl has bigger balls than I do.* "I hid in the cave and fell asleep then there was a huge lightning storm. I woke up when all the rocks crashed."

On closer inspection, Micah could tell that a big section of the mountain had broken free, creating the gap between him and the cave where Chloe was hidden. She'd walked into the cave and hadn't been able to walk out, unless she was some sort of New Age Jesus.

"Well, you're very brave, Chloe," he said, testing the rope one more time. "I'm coming over now, okay?" And before she could answer him, he began the slow, one-foot-in-front-of-the-other walk across the large yawning mouth of the valley. He didn't dare lift his feet, but rather scraped them along the mountain's edge, making rock and dust crumble, and he gritted his teeth to keep from following their path with his eyes.

He'd been working for Lewis and Clark County Search and Rescue Team for nearly six years and he never got over that feeling of being suspended over the incredibly far valley below. Even two decades later, memories still plagued him, very nearly paralyzing a man who was otherwise incredibly good at his job.

But before Micah could give in to any of those fears or panics, his feet touched down on the other side, grounding him against the dirt and mossy leaves, and there he was, at the entrance to the cave.

"Chloe," he called, his voice soft and gentle. "It's me, Micah. Do you want to come out of there now?"

She emerged, her movements slow and wary. Her clothes were dirty and her hair had all manner of sticks and leaves tangled in the curls, but she appeared otherwise unharmed, and Micah let out a low breath of relief. "You did a good job hiding here, honey," he said. "Now, I'd like to bring you home to your mom and dad, okay?"

She nodded and sniffled. "Okay." It seemed that the bravery that had gotten her so far was just about tapped out. Well, fine, she was allowed to be a kid again. It was no longer her responsibility to get home safely.

"Okay," he repeated. "Now, I'm going to hook you into this harness, then we're going to slowly walk across that gap. My dog, Axel, he's on the other side, waiting to meet you."

She nodded and, before either of them got the chance to freak the fuck out about trekking across that massive drop again, Micah had her hooked into the front section of the harness built for rescue missions just like this one, and he was scooting them alongside the mountain's sheer face, shuffling his feet and trying to keep breathing.

Then, mercifully, they were back on solid freaking ground, both inhaling more breath than necessary. Micah slowly, carefully, stood and picked Chloe up, hoisting her onto his hip. He unhooked the harness from the tree and whistled for Axel to follow before beginning the trek back up the hill to where their point camp was located.

It only took a few minutes. Axel kept a good pace and Chloe weighed about as much as a couch cushion, and before he knew it, the blue tent from their rescue rendezvous camp loomed into sight. A brief, weighty silence stretched across the mountain. Then all hell broke loose.

Her mother screamed then both of Chloe's parents were sprinting toward them, Police Chief Cade Easton and two of his deputies hot on their heels. Mr. Robinson took Chloe from Micah's arms and both of her parents were hugging her and touching her and making sure she was still in one piece. Micah tried to fade back, but Chloe grabbed the arm of his windbreaker.

"Thank you, Mr. Micah," she whispered, her bright eyes shining. Her parents both looked up at him with the same glowing adoration.

"Thank you, Micah," Mrs. Robinson said, as Mr. Robinson stuck out his hand and shook it hard, before bringing Micah in for a bear hug. Then they were gone, carrying Chloe over to the medic tent, and Micah stepped back to watch them walk off into the distance. He should have been relieved. They hadn't expected such a happy ending for Chloe and they'd been lucky, more than lucky.

But still, the ache in his chest didn't dissipate and he knew it was no longer fear that made him feel so heavy and forlorn. Axel whimpered at his side, and Micah dug into one of his pockets to give the dog a treat. He loved Axel and Rosie and the other search dogs they kept at the Black Reef Survival Camp, but dogs were a poor substitute for family, for parents, for children, for *people* who loved a person unconditionally. Well, dogs were what he was going to get, a truth he'd come to terms with a long time ago. Family wasn't in the cards for him, not the kind of family Chloe Robinson had. No, Axel and Rosie, they were what he got, so he'd damn well better be happy about it.

"Hey there, Superman," Dec said, coming up behind him, Rosie hot on his heels. "Or should I say Spider-Man? That was some gravity-defying shit you did down there."

And Dec McCormick. Of course. He counted as Micah's business partner, search partner, family and best friend, all rolled into one not-giving-a-damn package of good-old-boy humor and charm. Dec was one of the few people in the world who knew just how much Micah hated heights, but, as with most things, he played to the lighter side of the situation.

"I can't be out-balled by a six-year-old," Micah said, suddenly feeling very weary. He followed Dec away from the camp and toward their cabin a little way down the mountain. If Cade needed them to give statements, he knew where to find them.

"Ain't that the truth," Dec said. "Come on, let's get a beer."

Micah nodded, but glanced back up at the Robinson family one more time. Growing older with a houseful of dogs and their business and Dec McCormick by his side definitely wasn't the worst life a guy could have.

Chapter Two

"Madison..." Lily hoisted her duffel bag higher and shouldered her way into the kitchen. When she'd called her sister to ask if she could use the Triple Diamond Ranch for her research project, Madison — Maddy, as she went by now — had been overjoyed. Lily had been pretty freaking happy herself. Not a month after sending the email to her once-upon-a-time research advisor, Lily had gotten the go-ahead to start a new project.

She had been one semester away from finishing her master's thesis, a single research project she had never started away from getting her degree when the shit had royally hit the fan. It had been five long years, but Lily had a hunch that Montana had something good waiting for her, and Maddy had been all too willing to accommodate. She'd even mentioned a Welcome Lily party she was arranging, not that Lily needed anything of the sort. Still, she'd been out of the city just long enough to hop on a plane and drive from the airport, and already her mind had calmed some of its maddened racing and her chest had loosened a fraction of an inch.

It was a start. Though she was more than happy to see her sister, who had officially moved out to the ranch at the end of June, a little over three months earlier, the fact that Lily had brought her field kit, from which she had literally had to dust an inch-thick layer of grime, meant that this wasn't entirely a social visit. Or an easy one. The last time she'd opened that kit, Daniel had still been alive. The last time she'd gotten knee-deep in the dirt, instead of just finger-deep in flowerpots, she'd still believed he had a chance.

But this painful step was also a necessary one. She had left the flower shop in the capable hands of her best employee, Mia Halton, and taken three weeks of leave to both see Madison again and set up Wolf Creek, Montana as her research camp.

It certainly was beautiful. As she backed through the swinging kitchen door to the much smaller of the two main houses on the estate — the larger one, Holmwood Manor, having been converted to a B&B over the summer — Lily stared out at the grounds. The air was crisp and fresh, the sky wide and the far-off mountains a rainbow of golds and reds and fiery oranges. Nothing could beat fall in the mountains. Even if the research element didn't work out, she could at least enjoy her time away from the city.

But first, to find her errant sister.

She dropped her duffel in the mudroom and pushed through the door to the kitchen. And stopped dead in her tracks.

Madison was there, all right.

She was sprawled out on the counter, her mouth wrapped around one man's cock and her fingers tangled in the dark head of hair currently buried between her spread thighs. *Holy fuck. Oh, holy fuck. Jesus fucking Christ on a chocolate cupcake.*

Logically, she knew she needed to leave, but her feet couldn't seem to figure out how to move and, for a moment, Lily just stayed planted where she was. Madison had an…unorthodox relationship with two of the men who worked and part-owned the ranch, as she had explained over the phone on several occasions. Lily wasn't one to judge her sister's decisions, given her own veritable vow of celibacy, but to see the truth of her relationship with the two men right before her eyes was startling. Shocking, even.

And a little bit erotic, too…especially when the blond man buried his hands in her hair and tugged her head down, a low moan of pleasure caught in his throat.

No. Not erotic. Madison could keep her two lovers all to herself, because Lily didn't want any part of that kind of way-too-much-work relationship. She'd take her flowers over those kinds of complications any day.

Finally, somehow, her feet unglued themselves from the floor and Lily darted through the kitchen door, back through the mudroom without pausing for her bag and out into the yard. She threw a glance back at the house, as if expecting it to somehow look different from the outside. She was so distracted by the scene she had just witnessed that she didn't pay any attention to where she was going — until she collided head first into a wall.

A very muscular wall. A very muscular, solid wall that appeared to be *laughing* at her. Had she taken a wrong turn at Helena and ended up in Wonderland?

"Are you okay?" the wall asked and Lily got enough sense knocked into her cracked-out brain to tilt her head up and look the wall in the eyes. Of course, it wasn't a wall, but a man. A dark-skinned, dark-eyed man with black hair that came down past his shoulders and caught on the wind, whipping dramatically. He looked to be full Native American, with thick, slanting cheekbones that made her revise her statement. He wasn't a wall—he was carved from a freaking mountain.

And Jesus Christ better stay on that cupcake, because this man is sexy as hell.

Lily swallowed, her mouth dry and her eyes wide and unblinking. She took a step back, hoping that the distance might knock more sense into her totally overloaded brain and...*you've got to be fucking me.*

A pair of strong hands steadied her around the waist and she took a deep breath before turning around to face the other person.

Montana definitely had something in the water. Because the man standing behind her was the stuff cowgirl fantasies were made of. His skin was golden tan and matched his burnished-brown hair cropped high above the ear—a military cut grown that had grown out just a bit. He wore a pair of low-slung jeans with a loose flannel shirt tucked right behind the big belt buckle and Lily had to fight really hard not to picture exactly what was inside those jeans.

Had she lost her damned mind? Honest to God, she hadn't thought of another man in over five years and here she was, eyes popping out of her head at the sight of these two strangers—one of whom still had his hands around her waist. Fucking Madison and her fucking... Well, her fucking.

Finally, Lily stepped out of the line of fire of both men and stumbled a few feet away, where she was at last able to get in a deep breath.

"I think it might just be raining city girls this year," the cowboy said, a slight chuckle to his low voice. Lily bristled. She'd spent more than her fair share of time in the dirt, thank you very much.

"I take that to mean you're referring to my sister," she said, but her voice came out just this side of husky and there was a definite blush warming her neck and cheeks. She hadn't had a day this off-kilter in a long time.

"That must make you Lily Hollis," Tall, Dark and Mysterious said, holding out one large hand in her direction. Lily took a tentative step forward and shook it.

"I am," she said slowly. She eyed them both with obvious suspicion. "How do you know?"

"'Cause your sister has been telling the whole town you were on your way for a month," Mr. Charming teased, his hazel eyes twinkling at her. He really was...pretty, in a head-taller-than-her, built-as-hell, five-o'clock-shadow sort of way.

Lily couldn't help the low, derisive laugh that escaped under her breath. "Well, she's damn right happy at the moment, but it's not 'cause I'm here."

Both men's expressions contorted in confusion and Lily finally felt as though she were getting some grasp on the situation. A little, tiny fraction of grasp. Goddamn, had she *ever* been around so much hot masculinity in her life? It was throwing her way, way off. *No, it's just the scene in the kitchen shorting out my brain.*

"Let's just say I won't be eating off the counters anytime soon," she said, trying to stuff the laugh back into her mouth. Now that she was no longer suffering the shock of seeing the threesome going at it right there in the kitchen, the whole thing had an edge of humor to it. And that niggling, complicated desire that had made her curious. But it was one hell of a bad idea to analyze what *that* meant.

Understanding dawned first on the mountain man then on pretty boy and in an instant the confusion fled their faces, replaced with sheer, unadulterated mirth. The cowboy spoke first, barely able to get the words out around his amused laughter.

"Welcome to the neighborhood," he said. "If you walk in on the three of them doing something they're not supposed to, you're officially part of the Wolf Creek clan. It took me two weeks after Maddy officially moved in. Micah here wasn't so lucky."

Lily turned to the man named Micah, the laughter around his eyes making a little of that foreboding mystery fade away, and raised an eyebrow. Micah rolled his eyes.

"I came down from the cabin to borrow some supplies. Found them in the barn."

Lily sucked on her teeth and tried to keep the laughter down, but it wasn't easy. Not only was the whole situation funny and weird as hell, but now that they'd established some common ground, Lily found herself already comfortable and at ease around these two incredibly handsome, devil-may-care men. Maybe it was just being out of the city, since no one was ever this nice in the city, but she had the feeling it was actually these two men, themselves, with their charming smiles and contagious laughter. She turned back to the cowboy.

"Where'd you find them?" she asked.

He raised a brow and a spark of the devil shot across his eyes. Even without him saying a word, she knew he was about to try to charm the pants off her. She'd seen that look before and, coming from this guy, she didn't doubt its success rate.

"Bed of Ryder's truck," he said on a grin, a thousand-watt smile spreading across his face. "They got the bed part right, at least, if nothing else."

It took a minute for the three of them to compose themselves, but soon the laughter subsided and Lily got a deep breath in.

"Okay, okay. I'm glad I'm not the only one who got a private show, then," she said, clutching at her side in an attempt to alleviate the cramp all her laughter had caused. "I was a bit disoriented when I ran into both of you, so let's start again. I'm Lily Hollis and that promiscuous wench in there is my sister." A flash of the image she had walked in on crossed Lily's mind and she wondered, for the briefest of seconds, what it would be like to be the kind of promiscuous wench who fucked two gorgeous men on the kitchen counter.

It would be bad, Lily. Very bad. Shut that dirty trap of a mind.

"Welcome to Triple Diamond, Miss Hollis," Micah said. "I'm Micah, Micah Ellison, and that's Dec McCormick." He tilted his head in the other man's direction. "We run the Black Reef Survival Camp and work animal search and rescue for Lewis and Clark County from the compound just up the mountain. We're here for your welcome to Wolf Creek cookout, but I think Maddy and those vagabonds did a pretty good job with the whole welcoming thing."

His smiles were subtle, subdued, nothing like the broad, charm-the-pants-off-ya smile that Dec was now giving her, but, *oooh*, there was something to be said about the hint of danger and mystery at the edges of those dark eyes, even sparkling in amusement. These men, for all they were different in looks and initial personality, were undoubtedly cut from the same wicked, tempting cloth. *Not why you're here, Lils.*

"Thanks, I think," she said on a laugh. "I'm not quite sure what to do with myself now, since I can't go into the kitchen..."

"Now, you drink." Dec indicated the box of beer at his feet. "Come on, we can get the fire started while those guys screw on the kitchen counters..." He said it like it was so totally normal that Lily couldn't help but ask, following the two men toward the fire pit located on the back patio.

"So, is everyone just...like, cool with this? I mean, I'm from San Francisco, so I don't judge, but Wolf Creek seems like a pretty small town..."

Dec put the box of beer down at the edge of the large stone fire pit and nodded. God, her skin vibrated with each step Micah took closer to her, his presence like the smooth, thick caress of honey over her fingers, just as Dec's was the spice of whiskey on her tongue. That scene in the kitchen must have screwed with her head even more than she'd thought it had. She hadn't thought anything like this in *years*.

"It's a bit unorthodox," Micah said, settling several large logs into the fire pit and arranging them in a cabin formation. "I mean, personally, not my cup of tea, right? But Ryder and Christian..." He paused and pushed some of that silky dark hair out of his eyes to look up at her. Lily's heart stopped, just for a moment, at the sheer masculinity of the movement and she wrestled her wicked subconscious back to focus on his words. "But those guys are completely cooked when it comes to your sister," he finished.

"You should have seen them back at the fair over the summer," Dec cut in, handing her a beer from the box then giving one to Micah. "We broke up some big fight they were having before all three had their 'come to Jesus, I love you' moment. Ryder and Christian did a real number on each other. I'll tell you one thing, they'll do anything for Maddy and I think that sits all right with the folks around here."

He practically threw himself down on a cushioned bench seat near the fire and nodded to her. "You're allowed to sit. You must be tired from traveling and I can promise you won't find any more kinky orgies going on over here."

Lily laughed and walked over to the bench seat, settling against the arm and as far away from Dec McCormick as possible.

"Ain't that a shame," she murmured, before taking a long sip of beer. It was crisp and refreshing and hinted at apple and October spices. Of course, it wasn't nearly good enough to distract her from the weight of two very intense gazes homing in her direction.

"Something you wanna tell us, honey?" Dec's voice was way too smooth and charming, and he even managed to make that usually trite term of endearment enticing and decadent, but Lily just laughed. God, she'd been laughing more in the half-hour she'd been out in Wolf Creek than she could remember in a far too long time.

"I'm teasing," she said, suddenly not so convinced she was. Neither man appeared all that convinced, either. "Honestly, the guys I was with in college were enough work all on their own, thank you very much. I can't imagine having to deal with all that testosterone and ego twice over."

Micah's face appeared to sculpt before her very eyes, transforming from intensity to amusement.

"Dec and I skipped college," he said, innuendo thick and heavy in his voice.

Christ on calamari. What the hell was that supposed to mean? Because, whatever it was intended as, Lily's mind was on a whirling loop of some decidedly un-celibate images that had nothing at all to do with the awkward fumbling of her early partners.

But before the silence between them could stretch any further and before Lily could ask exactly what Micah had intoned in that rich and deep voice, all edged in mystery, and before she could do something really stupid like inch closer to the hot-as-the-bonfire Dec, the back door of the house swung open and Madison came running out.

"Lily!" Her hair was a mess and she had missed a button on her flannel shirt. Even if Lily hadn't witnessed the ever-so-graphic welcome of her sister on the kitchen counter, the truth would have been unmistakable.

"Mads!"

But Lily didn't care. Unorthodox relationship or not, if what Dec and Micah had said was right, then Madison's lovers made her happy and where Madison was concerned, that was the only thing that mattered to Lily. Given the incredible post-coital glow around her sister's smile, Lily had no doubt that she was doing more than just fine.

"How long have you been here?" Madison—damn it, Maddy—asked, pulling back to look her over. "God, I'm so happy to see you. So you've met Micah and Dec?" She indicated the two men sitting around the fire pit.

"Oh, yes." Lily couldn't help herself. "They were just explaining to me how it's a Triple Diamond welcome to witness you guys defacing the furniture."

Micah tried valiantly to stifle a laugh and Dec didn't bother, almost spewing his beer across the patio. Maddy blushed bright red and her eyes nearly popped out of her head. Montana had changed her sister, no doubt about that, and yet, Lily hadn't seen Madison look so relaxed, so at ease, in a long time.

"You saw that?" she asked, clearly knowing the answer.

"Pretty sure NASA has satellite images of that," Lily responded. "So stop stalling and introduce me already!"

Maddy's blush didn't dissipate, but she did turn around and indicate that the two men who had been standing a little awkwardly by the back door should come join them. Lily didn't blame them. The first Meet the Family sesh had gotten off to a rather graphic start, after all.

"Lils, this is Ryder and Christian," Maddy said, gesturing to a handsome blond man first then the man with dark hair and tattoos peeking out from under the wrists of his worn leather jacket. They were both large men and Mr. Badass especially would have intimidated her if they both weren't wearing such hang-dog expressions on their faces.

Lily couldn't help it. She laughed out loud then walked up to first Christian, then Ryder, giving them both large hugs, which, judging by their slack-jawed expressions, came as a surprise to both men.

"You guys make my Mads happy, so I don't give a damn what you do on the kitchen counter," she said. "And so what if it's a little unusual? Not my place to judge." She grimaced. "Just promise me we can eat outside while I'm here."

The two men relaxed a little, then Maddy poked Ryder in the chest. "We have people coming over and you promised me a real cookout, so get moving." She turned on Christian. "You too."

"What can I do?" Lily asked, feeling more at ease, at *home* than she'd felt in a long time. Being around

Madison had that effect. Or maybe it was all this fresh, crisp air and open sky. Of course, it couldn't be anything else.

"Nothing," Maddy said. "Just watch the fire and try to pretend Dec's not hitting on you."

"I heard that, Sweet Cheeks," Dec called from his spot on the bench. Maddy just rolled her eyes.

"Honestly. But don't worry, we prepped yesterday so there's not much left to do. I told a few friends to arrive around fiveish, so we're right on schedule."

"Except for these two bums," Christian said, as he unfolded a table and placed it on the lawn near the patio. "Did you get bored playing fetch?"

"I could teach Rosie to ride your Harley better than you can," Dec replied, a glint of excitement in his eyes. Oh, yeah, he liked tempting the beast, there was no doubt of that. Micah had the same fire in him, too, but his was all stealth where Dec's was all flash.

"Children," Maddy cut in. "The party, please."

Christian grumbled and shot Dec the middle finger before going off in search of more booze. Maddy hadn't been exaggerating about how fast she could get the party going, and not twenty minutes later, burgers were sizzling on the grill, hot, spiked cider and cold beers were out on the table beside a dozen sides and people were streaming up the dirt road to the ranch.

Maddy introduced Lily to all of them. Georgie, who couldn't have been much older than Lily herself, owned a ranch a few miles down the road. She wore her hair in a thick, messy braid that matched her messy smile and Lily liked her in an instant. She also liked Darla, who owned a B&B in town and came armed to the teeth with fresh desserts. Elsa was Maddy's first call for wedding cakes, Cade was the Chief of Police, Mary Lou and Deana were school teachers, Sawyer, James and Austin were firefighters... The list went on until the entire patio was filled with people, all expressing their excitement at meeting the famous Lily Hollis.

It didn't take long for the party to hit full swing. Maddy switched on several strings of lanterns over the patio and Micah got the fire really roaring as drinks flowed and conversation came easy. All these people, successful in their careers, happy in their home in Wolf Creek, they all seemed perfectly...*fine* with Maddy's arrangement. No one even murmured an ill word under their breath, not when Christian wrapped his arm around Maddy's waist or Ryder kissed her full-on in front of the fire team. It was kind of amazing. Maddy had found her community here, men who loved her and a town, at least, a large portion of a very small town, who supported her and her family. It was kind of incredible and Lily's heart filled with warmth and joy for Maddy and the new home she had found on the Triple Diamond Ranch.

"You're looking awfully introspective for a woman with a party being held in her honor."

She felt his presence before she turned around, but Lily would have known from a mile away that Micah was standing just behind her, having come out from the house with a new case of beer.

"Something on your mind, Lily?"

She had been trying to ignore him. Hell, she'd been trying to ignore Dec, too, if she were being honest with herself. But even with all the madness of the party and meeting new people and the music and the drinking, she'd been so aware of both of them through the whole night, of the intensity in Micah's eyes as he stoked the fire, in the seductive humor that Dec clearly used to keep his demons at bay. She'd barely known either of the men an afternoon and, yet, she couldn't deny the feeling of *knowing* them.

Which is completely absurd.

"I'm just thinking about how happy I am for Maddy, is all," Lily replied, finally looking up at Micah's half-shadowed face. "She really has a life here. I can't think of anyone who deserves it more."

Micah had a slow, wide smile and, try though she might, Lily couldn't ignore the way it made her feel, like the taste of hot cider, like the warmth of the flames licking her skin. This was freaking nuts. She hadn't so much as looked at another man in *years*, and now she had a case of the hots for *two* of them. *Note to self — don't drink the water in Wolf Creek.*

"What about your life in San Francisco?" Micah asked and, damn, if that low, knowing voice didn't suddenly make her want to spill her every secret. "Maddy says you run quite a successful business."

Lily had to smile, watching Maddy and her friends dancing to the music against the autumn night.

"She's always been my biggest cheerleader," Lily said. "My parents are in San Francisco, but we're a small brood. Ever since Madison left, it's been different." *Lonely.*

"You could always follow her," Micah said. "This part of the world could use a smile as bright as yours."

Then he was gone, slipping back into the party's rhythm without another word. Leaving San Francisco, returning to her research — it was already complicated enough. Surely she didn't need to go about adding honey-rich voices and burning-hot smiles to the mix. And yet, as she watched first Micah then Dec from across the patio, Lily had the feeling that she might already be too late to stop it.

Chapter Three

God, she was pretty. Dec McCormick's vocabulary really didn't run this side of *pretty*. He'd admit it to himself, if no one else, that he went for the crude, R-rated, T & A version of things. *Hot, sexy, stacked.* Pretty was for poets and men who didn't get laid.

Ha. And when was the last time he'd put any serious effort into getting laid? Sure, he kept up the flirtatious, charming thing because it was fun and a pretty easy spiel to fall into, but when it came to getting laid...he just hadn't cared. He could pinpoint the day he'd stopped caring, too. Eight and a half months ago, almost to the day.

But none of that changed the fact that Lily Hollis, now twirling her sister around the patio in some makeshift dance floor and laughing at something Georgie Jean had said, was pretty. *Really pretty.* She was slighter than Maddy and a little taller, too, with long, dark-brown hair that she had pulled into a messy ponytail. Her pale skin was dusted with freckles and her green eyes sparkled when she laughed. Hell, even her laugh was pretty and that was something Dec had never thought he would hear himself think in his entire life — and he'd nearly gotten engaged.

The thought was so sudden and wrenching that Dec almost spit his beer all over Cade Easton, who was sitting next to him glowering at Sawyer Matthews across the patio. Whatever. Dec had enough of his own drama and he definitely didn't need to delve into whatever bad blood had been between Sawyer and Cade since the summer after they'd all graduated Wolf Creek High School together.

He pushed away all thoughts of his not-marriage and his not-getting-laid and the half-growling police chief sitting behind him and focused again on Lily Hollis. She was sipping a fruity drink, sangria maybe, and her eyes widened at something one of the other women said, her mouth pursing around the straw in it. A guttural sound lodged in his throat at the mere suggestion of what else that mouth might be capable of.

Nothing, asshole. Right, because pursuing Lily Hollis was pretty much right at the top of the Dumbest Ideas Ever list. Not only was she Maddy Hollis' sister and all around best friend, something Maddy made no secret of, but she was also temporary. She was visiting, nothing else. She wasn't going to stay.

Just your type then, Dec...

Either way, getting involved with Lily could only lead to disaster. He wasn't an idiot. He'd seen the spark of desire in her eyes, though Dec hadn't quite figured out if it had been directed at him or Micah. Hmmm, nothing a little persuasion couldn't fix. If he wanted it to. Which, he was surprised to find, he actually did.

Dec glanced at the dwindling party, at Georgie and Darla and Elsa and the others. They were smart, beautiful women who were more than capable of holding their own. Hell, Georgie had a ranch and Darla and Elsa ran their own businesses. Wolf Creek had some badass women, that was for damn sure. And, yet, not a one of them stirred the same reaction in him as that very first sight of Lily Hollis had, a reaction growing stronger with every minute he watched her.

Folks started leaving and even the goodbye hugs and pecks on the cheek didn't make him feel a damn thing. Right, 'cause he hadn't felt a damn thing in eight motherfucking months and the fact that he was feeling it now was not uncomplicated.

He grabbed another beer from the cooler at his feet and saluted the fire station team goodbye before taking a long drink. The stuff was good. A new brewery had opened on the outskirts of town, run by two brothers, if he remembered correctly, and they knew their beer. He wasn't opposed to getting to know their beer very intimately tonight, either.

It was just... Jesus, it was just that he, the veritable flirt, charmer, bad boy, hadn't actually wanted a woman since Aubrey and though he was happy to find that his dick hadn't just shriveled up and died, this was...complicated. Plus, if he so much as pursued Lily Hollis, he'd have Madison's two very large, very protective bodyguards to deal with. And he'd take *them* over a set-down from Maddy herself any day.

"Where is that famous McCormick smile?" *Speak of the devil and she shall appear by your side with a tipsy smile and danger in her eyes.*

Dec raised an eyebrow. "Sweet cheeks, you know if I so much as look at you, those retrievers gonna come a runnin'." And, sure as shit, he could see Christian and Ryder on their way over to the fire pit where he and Maddy sat. A quick glance around told Dec that most of the party had gone home and it was just the handful of them left. Great, just what he needed, a chance to get more intimately acquainted with the way sangria looked on Lily's lips.

"I'm going to tell them you said that," Maddy said, but her eyes held humor and amusement. "But, really, why the sulk? There were plenty of beautiful women for you to dazzle tonight."

Dec's smile felt forced. *Because I don't want any of them. I don't want anyone.*

Maddy's smile faded and she placed a hand atop his, dropping her voice to speak again.

"You know," she began, the amusement all gone from her expression and tone, "I had a bad time of it with my ex. I don't know what the guys have told you, but I found him in bed with another woman, less than a week after we got engaged. So, if you ever want someone to commiserate with, you know where to find me."

This time his smile, though wan, felt a hell of a lot realer. "That sucks," he said, shaking his head. "But thanks, Mads, I appreciate it." Of course, that didn't mean he was going to take her up on it, but the point remained. Before Dec could say anything else, though, a weight on the bench beside him caught his attention and he turned to see Lily smiling over at him. Shit on a stick, it had been hard enough just watching her from across the yard.

"Hell of a party, guys," she said, taking an unsteady sip of sangria from a still-full cup. Or, rather, refilled cup. "I appreciate the welcome."

Micah settled on her other side, snorting out a laugh as he did and something that sounded suspiciously like *the second welcome...*

"I'm just happy you're here," Maddy said, cuddled between Christian and Ryder on the other side of the fire pit. It should have been weird — hell, it had been, back in the beginning. But now Dec couldn't picture her without both of them, not for a second. They really were a package deal. "So when do you start your fieldwork? Do we get to laze around for a few days before you have to play brilliant scientist?"

Dec cocked his head to the side. "Fieldwork?" he asked.

Lily opened her mouth, but Maddy beat her to the punch. "Lils is finishing her master's in horticultural biology," she said. "She'll be out here for a while doing field research."

Dec's eyes widened. "You're getting your master's?" he asked, unable to keep the surprise from his voice. Jesus, she was pretty and smart as hell.

"I almost finished it five years ago," Lily admitted and it wasn't his imagination that her voice had gotten low, as if it were some sort of confession. "I just needed to complete one more independent data set for the degree. Anyway, this place is great for fieldwork." She dug her phone out of her pocket, exposing a sliver of pale skin below her shirt, and Dec had to work to resist the urge to growl. Maybe he was regressing — how much time in a cabin in the mountains did it take to turn a man into a bear?

"This is the *Tanacetum vulgare*," she said, holding up a photo of yellow flowers with bunched, disc-shaped heads. "My research team is investigating the properties of the soil it grows in because sometimes the flower is toxic when ingested and sometimes it's not. I thought I'd take a look around on horseback in the morning and see what I could find."

"Wait a sec — let me see that again." Dec held his hand out to her and she placed the phone in his palm, biting her lower lip with a confused expression. "Micah, take a look at this. We totally have this shit growing in the yard, don't we? Near the kennel and out by the ropes course?"

Micah took the phone and looked it over, nodding after a moment. "Yeah, that's definitely it."

"You're kidding!" Lily clapped her hands together, excitement taking over her pretty face and making her look five years younger, though she was plenty young already, especially for someone who was *going back to her master's*. "This is perfect! If you guys don't mind, I could come up sometime tomorrow and take a look?"

"You could stay the night."

The words were out of his stupid mouth before Dec had the chance to clamp his teeth shut. What the ever-loving fuck was he doing? Inviting Lily into their cabin, even though they more than had the space to spare, was tantamount to opening a church door and letting the devil through. Jesus Christ, he'd better go ahead and take a bite out of every apple in the orchard because there was no way this could be anything other than temptation.

"Oh, I wouldn't want to impose on you guys like that," she said, but there was just enough hesitation in her refusal for him to push.

"Not an imposition at all," he said, "we've got the spare room and you can get an early start, if you'd like."

She looked him square in the eye, a secret feminine power behind her large, green gaze. Then she ping-ponged back to Micah, who shrugged and offered her that half-smile Dec knew so many women fell so hard for.

"You can eat off our kitchen counter," Micah said in a low voice, unable to keep the spark of mischief from coming through.

"Hey!" Maddy shouted from across the fire pit, where she'd no doubt been canoodling in some fashion or another. Dec just raised an eyebrow at Lily.

"Ass-free counters," he said, ignoring Micah's very large eye roll. "Think about it…"

Lily tried to hold back a smirk and didn't do a very good job of it. Finally, she just grinned that mega smile that kept throwing him off his game.

"Fine." She dragged the word out. "But just for the one night."

But as she finished her drink and went inside to grab her stuff, Dec had the feeling that even one night in the same cabin in the mountains as Lily Hollis was a very dangerous freaking idea, indeed.

* * * *

Dec and Micah's cabin was straight out of an L.L. Bean catalog. When Lily climbed out of Micah's truck, her duffel bag slung over one shoulder and her research kit in her hand, she felt a little as though she'd stumbled into a stock photo of *people camping*. The cabin was large and rustic, flanked by pine trees on two sides and a gorgeous navy sky filled with stars shining high above.

"What's that building?" she asked, pointing to another, smaller cabin a little way away. Everything smelled rich and crisp, like fresh, chilly air and fallen, crunchy leaves and sweet, tangy apples. Running her own business had taken weekends, nights and any vacation days she might have had, and a rush of nostalgia for her college camping trips and adventures swamped her.

"That's where we keep the dogs," Micah said, "and half a mile down the trail is the survival camp ropes course and obstacle course and the bunker." He walked up behind her, his hands shoved into his jeans pockets, shoulders slung back. Oh, yeah, forget the mountain range and the night sky. She had pretty much the best view — views — in the world, watching him and Dec standing on the mountain as though it was their kingdom. *Christ on a cracker, coming here was a mistake, a really big mistake.*

"*Most* of the dogs." Dec appeared at her side. "And the horses. Axel and Rosie are spoiled brats, so they sleep with us." And damn it to hell, Lily had the sudden, flashing thought of exactly what it would be like to sleep beside one of these men. Both of these men. *It's just because you saw Maddy and her harem this afternoon, nothing more. Most relationships are a one-to-one thing.* The only problem was she couldn't seem to pick which one.

"So, what exactly is *survival camp*?" she asked, because it was safer to keep talking than to be left alone with her thoughts.

"We train teams and individuals in survival techniques," Dec said, shrugging. "Kids looking to go into the army or become rangers, search-and-rescue dog teams, people like that. It lets us both work S&R for Lewis and Clark County and keep working." His voice was calm and even, but Lily got the impression that this survival camp, whatever that meant, was just as much a labor of love as her shop back home in California.

She was distracted by the faint sound of dogs whimpering and followed the two men into the cabin. The interior was even more rustic and homey than it had appeared from outside, distinctly masculine and smelling of pine and rich coffee and brisk mountain air and warm flannel straight from the dryer.

It didn't hurt that two beautiful, smiling golden retrievers greeted them at the door, first looking to both Dec and Micah for command then turning all their attention to the stranger in the room.

"Ruffians," Dec murmured, his voice full of affection, as he rubbed the closer dog's head. "The one with the purple collar is Axel." He nodded at the dog, now pressing his wet nose into Lily's ear. "And this is Rosie." Lily would have sworn Rosie smiled when Dec said her name, then Rosie joined in the kissing. Lily laughed at the tickling sensation but didn't pull away.

"You could have just told me about the dogs," she said, "I can't believe you got me to stay here by promising clean counters."

Micah snorted and scratched Axel behind the floppy ear. "It's a surprisingly effective selling point, isn't it? But this old place hasn't seen any action in a good long time."

She was pretty sure her gulp was audible, but the door shut loudly behind her and neither man seemed to notice.

"Psh, you two, I don't believe that."

Because of the open floor plan, she could see Dec standing in the kitchen and he turned away from the open refrigerator to raise one eyebrow at her.

"I think that might have been a compliment." He held up a beer and she shrugged and nodded. The more liquid courage she could get, the better off she was. *Right.* Until she let that liquid courage send her on a very dangerous journey toward what she really shouldn't want right now and would definitely regret in the morning.

"You know it was," she said, sitting down on the couch before the fireplace and accepting the beer Dec held out to her. "It can't come as a shock to either of you that you're both handsome men."

Their laughs were different. Dec had the laugh of a blazing fire, hot and exciting and combustible. Micah's laugh was rolling thunder, low and rough and full. In that moment, Lily couldn't pick a favorite. *Fuck me.* No. *Jesus Christ on a candy cane, this is such a bad idea.*

"You're going to bloat our egos," Micah said, settling onto the couch across from her. "Not every day a woman as beautiful as you tells a couple of mountain dwellers they're handsome."

She'd always been a blusher and now was no different. Her cheeks heated red and she licked her lips before thinking better of it. Dangerous territory she was traversing here. Maybe just going to bed was the smartest option, removing temptation and all that.

The problem was, she kind of liked the temptation. It had been so freaking long since she'd felt anything even *resembling* desire for a stranger and here she felt it for two. If that wasn't reason to celebrate, if that wasn't a step in the right direction away from the shadow of grief that had been lingering overhead for so long, she wasn't sure what was.

"Flattery will get you everywhere," she said with a smile. "Side note, this place is gorgeous. How long have you guys lived here?" She glanced around the cabin, with its tall ceilings and handful of landscape paintings and cozy throw blankets.

"Just when the subject was getting fun," Dec replied. "And almost five years. Christian and Ryder helped us build it. Lewis and Clark County S&R is sponsored by the state, but we bought the land for the Black Reef Survival Camp from Mason, so we're just on the border of Triple Diamond property, if you can believe it."

Lily's eyes grew wide. "No shit." She stood up and looked out of the large picture window toward the sprawling dark world outside. "Maddy owns land up this far?"

"And more," Micah replied. "Your sister is a rich woman." And yet, that wasn't exactly the reason Lily had been feeling a little envious of Maddy all night. Of course, trying to psychoanalyze the reasons she *was* would be a very bad idea.

She turned from the window a little too quickly and lost her balance, suddenly feeling the three glasses of sangria she'd had at the party. With an undignified *oomph*, she landed right in Micah's lap, spilling beer down her shirt in the process.

"I think that's my cue to go to bed," she said, her voice a little shakier than she was expecting and even Lily couldn't pretend it was because of the drinking or the jet lag. No, it was the incredibly large, incredibly solid man she was currently sprawled across, the one who was looking down at her with a mixture of amusement and something deeper and far more dangerous in his eyes. A long strand of his ink-black hair fell across his eyes and Lily had to fight not to push it over his ear. *Red alert. Red alert.*

She was up and off his lap in a split second. "Which room should I drop my bag in?" *Christ on a cream pie*, her face was definitely flushing now. Part of her wanted to chug the rest of her beer down just to cool her body temperature and part of her knew that with all the testosterone making what was a very large room seem so incredibly small, there wasn't much hope for cooling down.

"Down the hall, first door on your right," Dec said. He stood up from the couch and grabbed her duffel bag and research kit from where she'd dropped them near the door. "Come on. I'll show you."

Not a good idea. Especially since Lily couldn't shake the weight of Micah's gaze on her, or the sensation of being pressed against those hard thighs after she'd fallen into his lap. She was having a hard time getting her bearings.

"I can find it," she said, grabbing her bags from him and plastering her face with an overly bright smile. "Thanks again for letting me check out the field options up here, guys! See you in the morning." Oh, yeah, she sounded like a nut, what with the pinched, high tone of her voice and that stupid smile. But sounding like a nut was far safer than letting Dec McCormick or Micah Ellison walk her to the room she was using in their house, in the middle of the night, with her defenses down. Because her defenses were clearly down. There was no other explanation for this madness.

Before either of them had the chance to respond, Lily escaped down the hall and into the first room on the right, shutting the door firmly behind her and pressing her back against the wood, as if that might keep out some of the whirlwind of madness swirling around just outside.

Coming here, to Montana, to her sister's ranch and unorthodox relationship, had already been fraught with complication, with memories, with all the reasons she'd left the field and started up the shop in the first place. She hadn't expected any part of this trip to be easy or straightforward.

But for the first time since she'd received Dr. Malachi's response email, Lily couldn't help but think that her return to the field after five years, her facing up to so many things she'd pushed down for so long, was all going to be a lot more complicated — for reasons she couldn't have ever expected.

Chapter Four

The sun rose early the next morning, or maybe she'd just gone to bed late, not realizing that there was an enormous picture window on the far side of the room until it woke her with brilliant streaks of golden and red, the same color as swashes of trees outside, breaking through the early fog. She pulled on her comfiest jeans and a flannel jacket, perfect for the crisp weather they'd enjoyed at the party last night, and headed outside, suddenly desperate to feel the wind on her face.

Streaks of sunrise were just creeping up over the far side of the mountain, lifting the shadows of the valleys below, and Lily caught a glimpse of the far-off roof of the Holmwood B&B down on Maddy's ranch, and the winding dirt road Micah had driven them back on late last night. She was still on San Francisco time, which was how she justified sleeping in until after seven, something that she as a business owner hadn't done in a long time.

But though she'd spent the day traveling and the evening partying with the wonderful folks of Wolf Creek, Lily hadn't been able to fall asleep until way too late the night before. She'd been exhausted, but her mind had whirled in loops and kept her awake, questioning, wondering, thinking.

A gust of wind whipped her hair and she closed her eyes to better feel the breeze and the soft, weak sunshine on her face, to better smell the crisp leaves and that bite of morning cold and the dirt below her feet. How had she gone so long without dirt beneath her feet and wind in her hair? Here, at the edge of this mountainside, looking over the great valleys and hills below, she felt a little part of herself clink back into place.

And, sure as she'd expected to feel last night, she finally fell over the fine line, giving in to the guilt she had been skirting around since sending the email to her research advisor over a month ago. There was a very good reason she hadn't left the city in months, a fact Mia had reminded her of when Lily fussed over the orders and the scheduling. A Rose By Any Other Name was her baby, her pride and joy...and yet, maybe it was the distance in miles or the distance in something else altogether that made that silly little shop in the middle of an asphalt jungle feel less important this morning.

Which transformed the tinge of guilt at the back of her mind into a full, gnawing weight, and Lily opened her eyes and sighed, the moment of joy in the face of such unabashed nature gone to the memories, as so many things before it had been.

So, she walked, turning her back on the views and heading toward the second cabin, where Dec and Micah kept their search dogs. Nothing like some puppy love to settle a bad mood. The grounds were beautiful as she followed a worn foot path around a small pond, sparkling in the early streaks of sun, and toward the open back door to the barn-like structure, styled almost identically to the one Dec and Micah lived in. Far off in the distance, she could just glimpse the wooden top of a manmade structure, likely the ropes course belonging to the Black Reef Survival Camp, but it had disappeared from view when she reached the barn.

She stepped inside, enjoying the rich scent of hay and grain and wood, but stopped short at the sight that greeted her.

Dec McCormick had one fine ass.

He was bent over one of the stalls, communicating with whatever animal was on the other side of the small gate, and his jeans stretched taut across his backside, making Lily temporarily lose all sense of where and who she was. Aphrodite would be honored to eat cheesecake off that ass.

The thought was so crude and unexpected that Lily choked back a surprised laugh, catching Dec's attention when she did. He pulled himself up out of the stall — a shame really — and turned to face her, a hint of a grin already tugging at his scruffy face. He wore a well-loved-looking fleece jacket, with hints of flannel sticking out from the bottom and even crazier than how intently she'd been checking out his ass a second ago was the thought of how Dec would be one great way to stay warm on a late October night.

"I thought I heard you come in," he said, wiping his hands on that delicious ass and indicating for her to come over. "Wanna meet the team?"

Grateful for the distraction, Lily walked toward the stall and saw a large golden retriever and six squirming little puppies. She bit her lip to keep from squealing, but damn, if that wasn't the cutest freaking thing she'd seen in her entire life.

"They're precious." She turned to look up at him, suddenly very aware of how close they stood, looking over the stall door, how she could reach out and touch his cozy-looking jacket, stroke the curve of his rough, stubbled cheek.

"Hard to believe someone just dropped them off on our doorstep, right?"

She gaped at him, indignation taking root in her gut. "You're kidding."

He shook his head. "Nope. We have to spay and neuter our rescue dogs, but I guess someone mistook us for an animal shelter, and dropped off half-a-dozen three week old pups and their mama."

They're better off here anyway. "How old are they now?"

"Just seven weeks," Dec replied. "We're nearly done weaning them off sweet Allie here and then we start training."

"That soon?" She loved dogs, all animals, but when it came to working dogs, like the kind used by Seeing Eye foundations or search and rescue groups she didn't know shit from Shinola.

Dec turned to look at her and damn the man for having eyes prettier than his butt.

"We need to determine who to keep on as search dogs and who to adopt out," he explained. "Some take to the training naturally. Rosie and Axel both did. Bella, too. Jasper" — he indicated a dog sleeping in the stall beside them — "was a late bloomer but caught up quickly. You do this job long enough, you start to get a vibe for who's going to work out pretty early on."

Lily cocked her head to one side. "How long have you been doing this job?" she asked, despite the warning bells going off in her head that getting to know this man, getting to know either of these men, deeper than friendly stranger territory would only invite trouble. And yet, she wasn't sure if she wanted to close the door on trouble just yet. It felt so good to actually want someone after so long.

"Over a decade, if you can believe," Dec said, as though he couldn't quite believe it himself. "Like Micah said last night, I'm just not the college type." He sighed. "I joined the military when I turned eighteen, CSAR, Combat Search and Rescue. Got a nice little medical discharge three years later." He smacked his muscled upper thigh, giving her all the indication she would get as to why. "Wasn't going to sit around, though. When my leg healed up, I began volunteering with the Helena S&R team, where I met Micah on a statewide search for missing twin girls.

"Round about that time, Micah had just left... Well, anyway, we were both floating around, looking for something. I don't think either of us knew what. Anyway, we got to talking about how neither of us would ever want to feel that helpless, ya know? Long and short, we found the girls and got so drunk celebrating that we started a business together.

"I used to come up here as a kid, grew up on the other side of town, but I'd disappear for days at a time and camp out here, and when we sobered up and realized that, hey, we had a pretty good idea on our hands, I talked to Mason, Maddy's uncle, the one who left her the ranch. Anyway, he offered to loan us the land until we could pay it off. We could never thank him for all that he did for us, that man. But we paid it off over the next few years, bringing the survival programs up to scratch and still working S&R, but for Lewis and Clark County. And now" — he look back down at the puppies — "well, here we are."

Lily shook her head. "You guys are pretty frickin' amazing," she said, not looking up at him as she spoke. Just as she'd expected, hearing more about this charming-on-the-surface man had only made her like him more. *Okay, fine. One step at a time.*

"Takes one to know one, Ms. Hollis," Dec said, with a difficult-to-decipher grin on his face. God, she was so close to him. If she wanted, she could tuck her hands into that comfy sweater's pockets and yank him to her, press her body to his and...

But before she had the chance to give in to any of the cracked and very unlike-her desires currently heating her blood, his phone beeped alarmingly in his back pocket. His face contorted and he shot her an apologetic smile, before glancing down at the alarm.

"Aw, shit, is it nearly eight already?" He sighed. "I have to go teach a rescue crash course at the police department a few towns over and I'm already late." Because in addition to all the rest, he taught classes to police officers. For *fuck's* sake. "Let's go find Micah. He can show you where you might want to start your fieldwork today."

Right, great idea. Nothing like two overwhelming, attractive men in her face in the amount of time it took to swallow a cup of coffee. She'd be just fine. *Right.*

* * * *

He'd just finished the chapter when he heard footsteps coming out onto the porch and Micah turned to see Lily Hollis standing near the door. Her dark brown hair caught the breeze and she gave him a shy smile before thrusting out one of the two cups of coffee she held in her hands.

"Dec saddled me off on you," she said. "Said something about *going off to play teacher* and that he's taking Rosie and if you need any help with the invoices to figure it out yourself."

Micah snorted. He accepted the coffee and indicated for her to sit beside him on the deck that overlooked the mountainside. Life wasn't bad, not by a long stretch, though his mind flitted with worry at just how often Dec had been working jobs, even the teaching jobs, alone. Last year, Micah wouldn't have thought twice about that. They both worked jobs alone all the time. But ever since March and the whole fiasco with Aubrey—well, he'd known Dec long enough to recognize the signs of working too hard to avoid thinking too hard.

But since he'd much rather be talking to the striking near-stranger sitting beside him, Micah momentarily pushed his fears about Dec to the back of his mind and turned to Lily.

"I certainly don't consider it being saddled," he said. "We don't get a lot of company up this way when the training is out of session and it's nice to have someone to share the morning with." He'd meant it as an easy, off-the-cuff comment, but, incredibly, he found that the words landed rough in his stomach, far truer than he had thought when saying them. Or maybe it was just her, with those deep green eyes, like the forest in the spring, that made him feel so terribly off-kilter. Him, a man who'd been able to find true north with nothing but a stick or the light of the stars since he'd been seven years old.

In a somewhat desperate need to add humor to the moment, he said, "The best good morning kiss I've had in a while came from this mutt right here." He stroked Axel's fur and the dog rolled onto his back, silently demanding more belly rubs. Micah complied. He was weak where the dogs where concerned. *And some women, apparently.*

"I know the feeling," Lily said. "I haven't shared a morning in a very, very long time." Her voice wasn't wistful. It wasn't even sad. It was...resigned. Very nearly accepting, as if she'd gotten her lot in life and she wasn't going to complain about it.

"Who did you used to share them with?" he asked. "Let me guess — did you marry some French artist who stole your heart then your savings and disappeared in the night?"

She laughed like the wind in the trees, like the soft light from the early sun catching the dew, and Micah found himself watching her, just watching her.

Which was...unusual. Of the two of them, Dec was the one known for his charming, flirtatious, playboy lifestyle. He never brought women back to the cabin, instead choosing to spend the night at their places in town, and Micah, if no one else in Wolf Creek, knew that, in truth, Dec hadn't done anything befitting his reputation for the better part of two years, not since he'd met Aubrey, and not in the eight months since.... Well, since.

Micah didn't do casual sex. Sure, he appreciated a beautiful woman as much as the next hot-blooded man, but getting his jollies and leaving had sour connotations to it that he just couldn't shake.

Everything from the book sitting on the table beside him to the fairly isolated life that he kept in this cabin in the mountains somehow came back to that, to a desperate need to reconcile a decision he still believed in. It was who he was and how he lived his life, and had been for the last nearly twelve years.

And yet, this Lily Hollis, with her soft, freckled cheeks and easy smile, smelling of sunshine and crisp morning air, she caught his attention. Perhaps a little too much.

"Did you just ask me if I was *married?*" Her voice tinkled like the wind in the chimes they kept hanging off the barn door. "To a French artist? You have quite the imagination, Mountain Man."

He raised an eyebrow. "Mountain Man?"

She squared her chin, which made her look young and defiant all at the same time. Damn, he didn't even know how old she *was*. She had said something about leaving her master's program five years earlier, but she looked too young for that and he figured it wasn't enough to go on.

"You don't really need me to explain that one," she said, before taking a long sip of from her coffee cup. Nope, not coffee. Chai tea, with hints of cinnamon.

"If I'm Mountain Man, what does that make you?" he asked, unable to keep the amused smile from his lips. She had that effect on people. He'd seen it the night before at the party. "And tell me you didn't find *tea* in this house."

Apparently the tone of his voice *had* been that incredulous, because she laughed, more of that same, floating chime that sounded a hell of a lot like freedom.

"I promise your masculinity hasn't been compromised," she said. "I bring a stock of tea with me wherever I go. I'm a bit of a caffeine nut, to tell the truth. And as for *my* nickname...." She rolled her eyes, thinking. "Mads used to call me Wild Flower when we were growing up. The flower part — well I guess that's pretty obvious, but I did use to be a bit of a wild thing. Drove her crazy, with all her spreadsheets and to-do lists and everything. She couldn't understand how I could ever just pick up and leave for a weekend without planning every stop on the trip, ya know?"

She looked back up at him, her green, slightly almond-shaped eyes sparkling with a hint of humor and just a little bit of danger. Micah couldn't explain the feeling, but he somehow knew that she hadn't sparkled like that in a long time. Well, Wolf Creek had that effect on people.

"Come on," she said. "You promised me flowers and I want flowers, so lead the way, Mountain Man."

He had to resist the urge to pick her up and toss her over his shoulder in a fireman's hold at the nickname she'd given him.

"You're a menace," he replied, swallowing the last dregs of coffee before grabbing his book and leading them back into the house. "I have the feeling we'll know exactly how you got your nickname before too long."

And yet, the wild fire within this woman, one that seemed to be kindling before his very eyes, didn't scare him, didn't make him want to turn tail and run in the other direction, the way he had wanted to in the past, when other lovers caught his attention. Sure, he'd had a handful of relationships over the years and the fact that he kept ending up back at the cabin, licking his wounds, well, that spoke volumes about how they had all ended, didn't it?

But not so with her. And maybe that he found himself glad Dec had invited her to crash at their place, or that he was happy to show her around the grounds, or that he wanted to see more of her smiling face, when she discovered something or teased him — maybe that was the most dangerous of all.

She followed him through the kitchen and he took their two coffee mugs to the sink while she ran to get her fieldwork kit. Then he led her out of the cabin and down past the barn, following a worn dirt path he'd taken ten thousand times in the nearly six years he and Dec had lived in the cabin. Though neither of them spoke, the quiet was comfortable and easy and when Micah turned around to see if she was still following him, he caught sight of her wide-eyed, dazed expression as she turned in every direction, gaze following the tree lines and slashes of mountain views that cut through the fall foliage. He was lucky, living out here. He took the sights for granted, but, of course, she came from the concrete jungle and all that.

"Why'd you stay in the city?" he asked, when the path widened enough for the two of them to walk side-by-side.

She didn't pretend not to understand. "It's a long story. A sad story. Suffice to say, I'm already feeling revitalized by being out here. I mean, how lucky are you guys, living in this paradise?"

He let the change of subject pass without comment and nodded. "Wolf Creek is a good place to call home. Up ahead, just there, that's where we'll find your flowers. Down there is one of our camping spots."

Her eyes lit and Micah couldn't help but find the contrast amusing. She *was* a wild flower, blossoming as she wanted, blowing in the wind, smelling of nature and sunshine. But she was also a successful business owner and a scientist getting her master's degree, which required hard work and discipline and determination, and that was one hell of a combination.

As they neared the location she might use for her research, something starkly close to nerves quivered at the back of Micah's neck. Because he knew that if the plant, whatever the hell Latin name she'd called it by, was the right one, then she'd be staying at their cabin for a lot longer than one night. If it was the wrong one, though...

They reached the large patch of flowers, similar to the one she had shown them on her phone the night before. He watched her intently, watched her eyes and the smooth, pale planes of her cheeks, watched the fidgeting motion of her fingers against her legs — then, it stopped. Just like that. Every twitch of her body, of her fingers, of her eyes, just stopped. And all started up again in a whirlwind, when she dropped the research case and halfway sprinted to the mess of orange and white flowers sprouting in wild chaos from the ground. She sniffed, she touched, she got down on her hands and knees to look at them from the bottom up, her whole body a mess of limbs and untethered excitement.

"This is amazing!" she said. "Wait until I tell my research advisor. God, Micah, thank you." And, without warning, she caught him in a strong embrace. He stiffened, but only for a moment, before embracing her back. Oh, yeah, he knew what Dec and Christian and Ryder would have to say about that, about him hugging this beautiful woman over a patch of wild flowers. But with her arms wrapped around his waist and her head just below his chin, Micah didn't give a good goddamn.

Chapter Five

She had dirt under her nails, in her braids and packed between her teeth. Her feet ached in the heavy hiking boots and her back burned in protest, having been bent and twisted for most of the day. She wasn't even twenty-seven and yet, with all of her joints aching — why on earth did her elbow hurt? — and her muscles screaming from abuse, Lily felt about seventy-seven instead. And, *Christ on a chrysanthemum*, she hadn't been this freaking happy in a long time.

She climbed the stairs to Dec and Micah's cabin and stomped caked mud off her boots, before slipping them off her feet one at a time and dropping them on a large rubber mat near the door. On second thought, she peeled her muddied, disgusting, no longer white or dry socks off her feet, too, and dropped them on top of her boots to be dealt with later.

The door squeaked as she pushed it open and she immediately met the delicious scents of dinner — fresh chicken and herbs, rosemary, thyme, cilantro. Her stomach growled and she realized that more than eight hours had passed since she'd eaten anything other than the granola bar she had stuffed in her bag.

"Look what the cat dragged in," Dec said from across the kitchen counter. He had a dishrag over one shoulder and wore an apron slung low over his hips. "I hope you're hungry, Indiana Jones. Micah is with the pups now, but he'll be back in a few."

She blinked, not quite sure how to reconcile the charming, admittedly sexy, rugged lumberjack type with the fact that he was cooking. Chicken. With spices.

"You can cook..."

"Twenty-first century, honey. I can cook and you can work and ain't that the dream?" He was teasing her, of course, but it had been so long since she'd thought about a relationship like that, a relationship of equals, one where she came home to someone who wanted to hear about her day and maybe even make it a little easier, that the idea took her off-guard.

"Aw, shit, you're not a vegetarian, are you?" Dec asked, misinterpreting her expression. "I know how you hippie types are."

"Hippie types?" she asked, a little dumbfounded. "And no, definitely not. It's just...unexpected, is all."

"You're definitely a hippie type," he said. "I bet you have pot brownies in your research kit." The statement was just dumb enough to unstick her face, and she coughed out a laugh.

"I do *not*."

He shot her *that grin*, the one that made her stomach feel a little hot and her face flush. "Only because you couldn't get them on the plane. Now, go wash up the entire mountain-worth of dirt off your body so I have something to fantasize about while I finish up dinner."

Coming from any other man, the statement would have been wildly offensive. But Dec McCormick had a way about him where she felt like she was in on the joke, and the depths she'd seen in those hazel eyes just that morning gave Lily all the proof she needed that he used humor as a way to deflect the sadness buried below. Still, she *was* covered in eight hours' worth of dirt, and she could feel it beginning to crust over on her skin, so she rolled her eyes and headed for the bathroom, and almost ran head first into Micah who was coming in through the back door.

"Whoa." Humor lit those mysterious eyes. "You leave any dirt at the research site or..."

"It's not that bad," she tried to defend herself. In the early months of her master's, she'd spent weeks out in the field, with only the occasional sponge bath. Micah cocked his head to the side and lifted one of those large, dark hands to her face, brushing a smudge of dirt off her cheek, his touch so, so gentle.

Her breath caught at the contact and for a moment they both stood frozen there, the touch between them barely a whisper and yet...*oh my.*

Then the silence was shattered by the unmistakable yelp of a tiny puppy that Micah had apparently been holding inside his flannel jacket, something she hadn't noticed because she'd been too busy craving more of that touch.

"Had to bring one of the little ones in," he said, breaking their contact as quickly as if he'd been burned and turning toward Dec in the kitchen. "Her back leg seems to be bothering her and I wanted to keep a closer eye. If it gets any worse, I'll talk to Ryder about it."

It was only because the puppy was so freaking cute, with those giant paws and floppy ears, and not because

Lily wanted to focus on anything in the world other than the way Micah's touch still lingered on her skin, that she cooed over the pup.

"What's her name?" she asked, her voice a tad too high for comfort.

"Doesn't have one yet." Micah shrugged, not quite meeting her gaze. Funny that, how a man as powerful and capable and strong as this one would shy away from looking at her over a simple touch. And yet...maybe that just meant he'd felt the same insane heat she had?

"Can I name her?" Lily asked, forcing her attention away from Micah.

"As long as we have right of first refusal," Dec called from the kitchen. "I swear, if you name her Fluffy or Princess or some other ridiculous name..."

"I would never!" Lily looked the puppy in the eyes and the dog seemed to smile at her, one ear tossed over her head, making her just about the freaking cutest thing she'd seen in her life. "Isn't that right, Cupcake?"

Micah laughed. "God, no."

"I'll think about it," she said. "Now, before I permanently become Dirt Woman, I'm off to shower. Or maybe I should just go hose off. I don't want to clog the drains."

"As much as I'd love the chance to hose you off," Dec teased, "the plumbing's all new. We come back from jobs pretty covered in nature most of the time, so don't worry about it."

She wasn't worried about it. What she was a little worried about was that Dec's words, meant as a joke though they had been, made her face flush a little. What she was worried about was that she couldn't get the lingering, featherlight touch of Micah's fingers off her skin. What she was worried about was that if anything were to happen, if she were to finally give in to a desire she hadn't felt in so many years, for *any* man, she was going to need to pick which one. And how on earth could she do that?

The shower was warm and inviting and she wondered about staying under the spray forever, never leaving the comfort and relative safety of the bathroom, which even smelled like the two men, like campfires and whiskey and strong coffee. Because this was complicated. Because Dec was out there cooking them dinner and Micah looked even more masculine while cradling a tiny puppy. Maybe it was just that being away from the shop, being back at work in the field, had opened something inside her, allowed the guilt and longing and memories to take a back seat, instead of driving her every choice and decision? Maybe it was the anniversary of Daniel's death, the simple passing of time, that had made all of this madness come to a head all at once? Maybe it was just Wolf Creek, because apparently wanting two men was pretty much par for the freaking course around here?

Or, more realistically, far more dangerously, it was these specific two men. It was Dec's humor and charm and hidden depths. It was Micah's mystery and quiet amusement and clear sense of morals. It was how they both made her feel, each in their own way, comfortable, safe. *Aroused.* She glanced up at the showerhead and sighed. That was the safer option than trying to sort out all her tangled emotions and desires right now.

She leaned back against the wall of the shower, a dark, slatted wood that smelled like nature incarnate and fresh air and freedom, and Lily let her fingers slide across her stomach, one hand going up to cup her small breast and one hand going down, to part her wet folds and slide her hand between to brush her straining clit. It wasn't smart. It wasn't a good idea to get herself off imagining the touch and feel and taste of the two men just down the hall. She shouldn't be imagining either, let alone *both*, but of course it was smarter, safer, to rid herself of the coiling tension that streaked every interaction she shared with them, either of them. *Both of them.*

Her nipple plumped between her fingers and she brushed across the straining bud, imagining what it might feel like to have Dec's mouth on her, or Micah's hard body, the one she had felt the night before when she had fallen into his lap, pressed against her back. Christ on...a *something*, she couldn't even fantasize about one man at a time.

So, she slid her fingers deep inside her body, swirling her thumb in circles over her swollen clit as she gave over to the fantasy of Micah burying his cock deep inside her, of Dec pressing his full lips to hers. Then, oh, *God*, it was too much, way too much and she peaked too fast and too hard and too high, biting down on her lips to keep from crying out as wave after wave of pleasure shocked her body, arched her back and had her breathing coming in hard pants.

Suddenly, the water in the shower was too warm and she cranked it to a degree just above ice, trying to cool her heated skin and overheating mind. Okay, so she wanted them. Both of them. Deep in the throes of passion, she could no longer ignore the truth of that. But she certainly didn't need to act on it. These men, the first she had thought of as *men*, as potential lovers, in so many years, could remain a delicious fantasy, a way to keep herself occupied on lonely nights. Of course, that didn't mean she had to give in to her desires. She was a grown woman, for goodness' sake. She could more than control herself around them.

Right. Right?

* * * *

"Hermione?" Lily said, looking down at the pup, who watched her patiently from just the other side of the kitchen gate, still visible from where they sat eating dinner.

"You're not naming the dog Hermione," Dec said, handing her a plate of roasted vegetables. "Or Harry or…I don't know…wasn't there a Robbie or something in those books?"

She cocked her head to the side. "Ron," she corrected, narrowing her eyes. "Are you telling me you've never read *Harry Potter*? You're shitting me, really?"

"Really," Dec replied. "I'm not…the reading type." He said it with bravado, but Lily couldn't ignore the hint of something below those sparkling eyes and her mind flitted back to all the nights her mom and dad had read Madison and her to sleep far too late.

"You could be," she said. "Being a reading type is just about figuring out what you like to read." She turned to Micah. "What were you reading this morning?" He'd been silent for the last few minutes, but she found that he was always watching, always listening, never far away as he looked like he might be. The man was perceptive as hell.

He blinked, taken by surprise. "Non-fiction," he said. "Historical." He coughed, clearly uncomfortable, but came clean, anyway. "*The History of the Battle of Belly River*." He shrugged.

She raised a brow. Stupidly, she had assumed that leaving his reservation had included some...she didn't know, lack of connection or some such to the world behind. Of course, that didn't make any sense and now that she thought on it, Lily felt a little ashamed. She turned back to Dec. "See? We read what interests us. So, what do *you* like?"

"What do *I* like?" He sounded a little incredulous and she didn't like the idea that maybe he wasn't asked that question enough. She nodded. "Well, cooking, but I'm not about to start settling down in the hammock with a cookbook."

"Fair." She indicated the food on the table. "Dinner is amazing, by the way." He only preened a little. "What else? Travel? History? Adventure? There must be something that tickles your fancy."

And there was that freaking grin. It wasn't so much the smile on his face as it was the one in his eyes, twinkling humor across the gold, streaked with green and molten brown, like melted chocolate, and she knew what he was going to say before he even opened his mouth.

"Oh, I could think of a few things that tickle my fancy," he said, dropping his voice an octave and in a clear charade of seduction. Yeah, right, the man could seduce a brick wall with a wink and a nod. He didn't have to fake seduction.

"You're incorrigible," she replied. She glanced back at the dog. "Casanova..."

Micah laughed at her side, and Lily felt that laugh like a caress, running down her sides, making her breathing heavy and her body ache. Despite everything that had happened in the shower, both the cleaning part and after, she hadn't been able to shake his touch from her skin, to shake the desire she felt for more than just a brush of fingers across her cheek.

"One is enough," he said. "I don't need a second Lothario in my life, thank you very much."

"I am not a Lothario!" Dec lobbed a mushroom across the table and Micah ducked out of the way, so it splatted on the floor behind him. Not-Hermione-Cupcake-or-Casanova barked from her spot in the kitchen. Rosie and Axel didn't even raise their heads, still asleep on the couch.

"You're right," Micah said, his voice apologetic. "Lotharios are usually more successful."

Lily just watched them, the comfortable banter, the easy camaraderie of brotherhood, because whatever had brought these two men together, and whatever kept them so close, even now, was clearly a bond as strong as any brotherly ties. She'd been lucky, growing up with Maddy and their loving mom and dad, though it hadn't always been easy, as Maddy had dealt with the loss of her parents and the uprooting of her life through the adoption. But they would always have a home, her and Mads, a place to return to when the going got a little tough. Lily couldn't deny the sensation she felt that neither Dec nor Micah shared that same comfortable hearth.

Out of the buried and locked corners of her mind, an image floated. It was such an aged memory, not just by time but by abuse and neglect, and the corners were faded and a little out of focus, but oh, *God*, she felt the truth of it right down to her bones, and all of a sudden it felt like she was *all* bones, a rattling skeleton of the woman who might have lived in that little house with the man she loved, if life hadn't all gone so terribly wrong.

"Lily?" Dec cocked his head into her line of sight and she blinked, confused to find that she was just a little watery, and no, God *no,* she was not going to cry, not here and not ever again. Coming out to the ranch to finish her fieldwork was a step forward, several steps forward, and she needed to hold onto the victory of healing and relief, not allow herself to fall back into the *what could have beens* that had haunted her for so long. "Honey, are you okay?"

Micah didn't say a word, but he was there, closer, his presence like the warm glow of the fire on a cold night. Both their gazes were potent and concerned, and she must have looked a mess to warrant such an incredible change of atmosphere in such a short time. But their caring, both of their caring, and the power that each of these two men had over her desires, which she still hadn't freaking figured out the why or how of, it wasn't helping, not even a little bit.

Coming here had been a mistake. She'd been drunk on sangria and October in the mountains and the freedom of being away from the shop that ruled her entire life, and she'd been weak, so happy to find that her desire, her base carnal longings hadn't deserted her completely, that she'd agreed to come up here, to be alone with these two men who confused the ever-loving shit out of her.

But it had been a mistake. Because, though she didn't look at either of them, she could *feel* them, sense them, almost see what they were thinking, and Lily knew she wasn't ready. Definitely not for *this,* probably not for being back at work or for even leaving her shop for a short time. How on earth had she thought she was ready, when the weight of her guilt and raw grief — God, weren't wounds supposed to heal over time? —

gnawed at her insides and made her suddenly feel sick to her soul?

She stood up abruptly and tossed her napkin to the chair, making for the hallway. "I need to go," she said. "I think I'm going to call Madison, stay down there tonight." She spoke with her back to the two men and the intensity of their gazes, their concern, only grew hotter and stronger. Neither of them made a move to stand, though, and for that she was incredibly grateful. If either man touched her right then, she wouldn't be able to hold back the barrage of tears just lingering right at the edge.

"Lily, what's wrong?" Micah asked. His voice was low, barely audible over the whirling of thoughts in her head, and she clenched her fists hard to keep from spilling over, with the crying, with the everything.

"I thought I was ready," she said. And yup, there was the sob, there was that banshee-like wail of air being sucked into her throat against the scratch of her tightening windpipe. "I don't know if I'll ever be ready..." The words caught, tangled in her mouth, in her mind, a truth so desperate and sad, so raw and painful, that she gave over to it, to the fierce sobs that caught in her chest and her throat. She didn't cry out loud, but shook, as if her body was trying to exorcise her demons. Well, it hadn't gotten the memo that those demons were here to stay.

"Can...can you call Madison?" she asked. "Please?"

"I already texted her," Dec said. "She's on her way up."

Lily didn't even care that he'd clearly called in the reinforcements at her moment of weakness. It was better that way, better that these men take their cues and leave her to disgusting, pitiful sobbing until Madison got there.

"Come on, Wild Flower." But Micah was at her side, not leaving, not giving her the space to stare down the empty, dark hallway, wondering what the ever-loving fuck she had thought to accomplish by emailing her research advisor that night. She turned back away from him, but Dec was only a few feet from her, leaning against the counter as if to give her an escape route, not to crowd around her. She hated that, hated that these two strangers, barely even *friends*, knew what she needed, even when she couldn't even tell up from down. Before she could muster enough extra air into her lungs to tell Micah to just leave her, to let Madison come up here and play clean-up crew, Micah slipped his arm under her waist and lifted her up from the ground, cradling her to his chest just as he had done with the still-unnamed puppy only a little while earlier.

"What kind of tea do you want?" he asked. "I know you have a stock in your bag. Dec will get you some."

She shook her head as he carried her over to the couch and made to place her down. Without conscious thought, she clung to his arm. Desperate as she'd been for him not to touch her, she couldn't imagine him letting go. But she didn't need to say it for him to get the message and, instead of depositing her on the couch, he sat down and held her in his lap, stroking her hair, her back, her arms, as if she were a child.

God, she felt like a child. She'd all but been a child five years ago, seven years ago. Seven freaking years ago. And yet, some days that time felt like a blip, a mistake in the continuum that had run through in double speed, so fast she'd barely seen it.

"Lemon," she managed under her breath. "Lemon's my favorite…" and why on earth were those the first words out of her mouth, when this big mountain of a man was holding her so close, not showing any signs of fear or frustration at her inexplicable breakdown. *Lemon.* It was the only rational thing she could focus on right now.

"On it," Dec said, and she watched him move down the hall out of her peripheral, in search of lemon tea, as if any of that would solve anything, as if lemon tea could somehow give her answers, peace. Daniel.

"God, I'm so sorry." She had to choke out the words, her throat still so swollen from the waterworks. "This is the worst way in the world to thank you guys for letting me stay here."

Micah pressed a chaste kiss to her hair and continued to stroke her back.

"Don't talk, Lily. Don't worry. It's all okay."

But it wasn't okay and she had to wonder if it would ever, ever be okay.

Before she could respond, though, the door to the cabin swung open, sending a huge rush of cool air into the room and Madison came running inside, panic stretching across her beautiful face.

She sat down on the couch beside Micah, doing her damnedest to hide her concern, but Lily knew it was there, just as Maddy knew exactly what was wrong. They were too close, too connected, to ever get away with hiding things from each other.

"Oh, sweetie." Maddy stroked her face, tears in her own eyes now. "Oh, my sweet Lily." God, but was there anything in the world better than the touch of a sister's comforting hand? Though Micah's strokes up and down her arm were definitely a close contender.

"I wasn't ready, Mads," Lily said after a long moment had passed. "I thought I was. I really did."

"It's okay," Maddy replied. "It's all okay. You were ready the day you requested to go back into the field and now you're feeling a little unsure. That doesn't mean all is lost, okay?"

The kettle rang out behind them, and Lily took a deep breath, the first dry one she'd managed since this whole circus had started. She took another, then another, then Dec was there, holding a cup of lemon tea, a schooled, unreadable expression on his handsome face. He handed it to her and she took the steaming mug, sitting up a little in Micah's arms to inhale her favorite scent.

Oh, *God*. Now that her little freak-fest was over, she was suddenly very aware of the mess she'd made. Her face felt tight from the tears drying on her skin and a steady, low drumming banged against her temple. *Pound, pound, pound.*

She'd been away from her shop for less than twenty-four hours and had completely lost her shit. Full-on panic attack meltdown. In front of Madison, who was watching her with carefully concealed panic on her pretty face and in front of Dec and Micah too, who had been fun and kind and a desperately needed reassurance that she hadn't lost her ability to desire a man, as she had honestly started to believe.

"I owe you guys an explanation," she said, half into her teacup.

Once, Maddy had called her brave. It had been toward the end and Lily had fallen asleep at her parents' house, waking in the middle of the night to terrors about hospital rooms and bright lights and the low, sad line that meant a heart had stopped beating. Maddy had been home from college and she'd woken to Lily's whimpering on the couch in the living room and she'd held her through the night, when the whimpering had turned to very awake sobbing for all that she hadn't yet lost, but was so clearly going to.

She hadn't cried that much in a long time, maybe even until tonight.

But Maddy had called her brave. Her big sister, once a dear cousin, who had survived losing both her parents at the same time, had called her brave. For staying. For continuing to love a man who was so close to the end.

Lily didn't feel very brave right now. Right now, she felt bone weary, in a way that had nothing to do with the hours she'd spent in the dirt that afternoon and everything to do with the pounding rush of guilt and fear and panic that had consumed her all at once at the dinner table. In San Francisco, back at the shop, she had found a way to keep those demons at bay. But all her defenses, all her excuses, all that she had so carefully constructed around her heart to keep her safe and sound, all that had shattered into a million tiny pieces the night she had emailed Dr. Malachi and told him she was ready to go back out into the field.

"You don't owe us anything," Dec said. He was standing behind the sofa, just over Maddy's shoulder, and he had a fierce, protective expression on his usually easygoing and cheerful face. An absurd thought crossed her mind in that instant, because Lily actually found herself thinking that she had never seen such an expression on Dec's face. *Never.* Right, because she had known this man less than a *day* and whatever illusions she had about something deeper and stronger and more powerful were illusions and nothing else.

Just like the illusion of how comfortable she felt in Micah's embrace, as if this wasn't the second night in a row she had ended up in his lap on this couch, and a whole lot less fun for it.

"We have to stop meeting like this," she said, looking up into his deep, mysterious face. He looked back into hers, holding her gaze, giving a taste of that same fierce protectiveness she had seen in Dec's. It was too much. But this time, it didn't set her off, not like before. This time, for whatever reason, Madison's presence or the screwdriver that had gotten Lily's head back on straight, she was happy that Dec and Micah were here, looking for all the world as though they'd do whatever it took to never see her cry again. *Head-trip alert.*

"I don't mind," Micah said. He leaned down and brushed a strand of her hair off her face. It had adhered to her skin with all the tears, and he tugged it free, brushing it behind her ear. "And Dec's right. You don't have to tell us a thing. But if you want to, we'll listen."

Lily felt, rather than saw, Madison glancing between the three of them and Lily just knew she was about to entertain one hell of a conversation with her sister when all the drama of the night had passed. But, for now, one problem at a time.

"The abridged version," she said, sitting up, because it was really freaking hard to concentrate on anything with Micah's powerful, muscled back pressed against her. "I skipped a few grades." She said this part on a laugh, as if any of it mattered. The ages and numbers and details sure as shit didn't. "So I was a senior in college when I was nineteen. It seems so young now, but I really loved him, I did. I *was* young, yeah, but Daniel, God..." She cut herself off, then squared her shoulders and lifted her head. If she couldn't even talk about this then how in the hell could she ever move past it, ever heal from it?

"He was diagnosed at the end of our last semester." She said it all in a rush. "He was supposed to go on, you know, had nearly a full ride to Colorado for his grad program and he would have been great." She let herself reminisce for the moment, let herself remember that day in summer when Daniel, then her lover and partner for over a year, had gotten the notice of acceptance to his top school. They'd been camping, when the email had come through, and had spent the night making love around the fire. "Hodgkin's Lymphoma..." *Deep breath out.*

"He didn't go." Dec said the words with the finality they deserved.

"No," Lily said, mouth still hovering over the lip of her teacup. "He didn't go. But he made me go. UC Davis was closer than Colorado, of course. He never said a thing, but I know he pushed because he wanted me to have something to hold onto when it all came to a head." She let out a low, derisive laugh. "Of course, I didn't finish the program, now, did I? One semester of fieldwork away from my master's and...I quit. Took my college money and opened the shop, just like we'd dreamed of doing."

She stood up, because all of a sudden the room was too hot and her comfy flannel was too hot and the weight of three sympathetic gazes was way too freaking hot.

"I panicked," Lily admitted. "I just... Going back to the field set me off, I guess. It brought me back there, back to those months where I kept wondering if it was going to be this weekend, while I was off in the Redwoods, or this weekend out on the Appalachian."

She looked from Micah to Dec, before finally landing on Maddy's knowing face. Of course it was knowing. Maddy had been there through the whole thing, the shoulder Lily had used on far more than one occasion. Maddy knew pretty much every sordid detail of the whole wretched affair and, by the expression on her face, she was remembering them in real time, just as Lily was.

"He proposed to me," she said quietly, rubbing the finger that would have held his ring, her husband's ring. If only she had been so lucky. "Right around Christmas. Two weeks later, I got the call that the final semester research site had been moved to Arizona and I...I quit. Right there on the phone. How could I spend three months in Arizona when my fiancé was...? Well, it turned out I was right."

Maddy stood up and walked over to her, determination in those fierce, glittering eyes, before she hugged Lily in a tight embrace.

"Shhh, now, sweetie. Don't rush. It'll come out as it needs to."

But it had been five years and one month and three days she had been mourning. Hell, it had been over six years, nearly, since she'd been fighting the same fucking fight, with hope and panic and drenched fear, and it needed to come out *now.*

"He died three days before I would have graduated." Her voice was strong, nearly unrecognizable, and Lily held her head just a little higher. "And I don't regret dropping out of school or opening the shop, not for a fucking second." She scoffed. "But apparently time doesn't heal all wounds."

"Time doesn't heal wounds," Dec said, from where he stood behind the couch, stance rigid, eyes blazing with something she just didn't have the reserves to deal with right now. "Time just makes you better at dealing with them."

She sniffed. "I'm not doing all that great a job dealing with them right now."

"You are, though," Dec replied, holding her gaze. "You've made a whole life for yourself, a business… After all that you had barely managed to make it through, you started a business. Most people wouldn't even consider doing something like that."

"It was Daniel's dream," she said with a sad fondness. "Toward the end, he got very involved in Eastern medicine, and flowers and nature, they called to him in a different way than they had when he was a scientist. We would spend hours just talking about the places in the world he wanted to visit and the plants he would import from South Africa or Brazil. So, I started the shop. For him."

"How long has it been since you've done something for you, Lily?" Micah asked.

She nodded. "I came here," she said. "I picked my research back up again." The first genuine smile of the night. "And would you look at that, I'm scared completely and utterly shitless. Daniel, loving him, caring for him, dreaming with him, mourning him—it's been my life for so long that…I don't know if I really remember who I am outside of his memory." *And damn, if that isn't the scariest thing of all.*

Chapter Six

Dec was up at three. He lay in bed for a long time, watching the sliver of moonlight that rippled through the trees, casting waves of shadows and brightness across his bedspread. He watched the moon and he breathed and he thought.

About Lily.

It had been three days since she had broken down at the dinner table and he hadn't been able to get the sight of her face, racked with grief and pain and guilt, out of his mind. And his heart ached, for her, for the girl — God, she'd barely been old enough to drink when the worst kind of thing that could happen to a person had happened to her. At nineteen, she should have been sneaking into bars and kissing the wrong sorts of boys, not caring for a dying fiancé who was not much older than she was.

His insomnia was getting bad again. Rather, it had been bad since March, teasing him, making him think that some nights he might actually be able to get some fucking sleep. But tonight, he didn't want to fall back to bed, at least, not right away, not when his mind kept flitting back to the beautiful woman sleeping just two doors down from him. *Alone.*

Of course, he knew how it felt to be alone, didn't he? All these twenty years later and he felt *alone* as keenly as his dad when his dear old mama had walked out of that trailer door and never looked back. Just because he knew it, didn't mean he liked it. Hell, any psych major worth half their salt could connect the dots between a grown man with mommy issues and the same grown man who picked up a different chick at the bar every night of the week.

Had. Before Aubrey. Before he'd almost gotten married.

Yeah, he'd been serious about it, too. Serious enough about marriage to drive the near ten hours to her home in Billings, North Dakota, where she lived when she wasn't working for her company's consultant firm in Helena, hell-bent on asking her to marry him. The house had been plain, white and blue, two stories, small garden, a house she'd never invited him to — a house she'd apparently shared with her husband and three kids.

It seemed that this week was fucking feelings-sharing time, because Dec felt heat at the backs of his eyes and pulled up and out of bed before he could stop himself. He yanked on a pair of flannel pajama bottoms and stuffed his feet into fleece slippers, because damn this cabin had cold floors, and he went to the kitchen.

¼ cup sugar, ¼ cup flour, 2 tbsp cocoa, 2 tbsp oil, 3 tbsp water, pinch of salt.

He mixed the handful of ingredients around in a coffee mug and popped it into the microwave, setting the time for a minute thirty. Then he pulled open the freezer drawer and...*score!* Two cartons of ice cream were pushed to one side and he grabbed the Oreo mix one before shutting the freezer door.

He'd be lying to himself, and ineffectively, if he claimed that he didn't want the brownie. Ever since he'd discovered mug recipes a few years back, he'd become something of an expert in them. But there was more to this now almost nightly ritual than just brownies and ice cream, not that he was complaining about that.

Cooking, and by extension baking, some of the simpler recipes, calmed him. Just like a really good run or hike through the mountains could help orient his compass, taking pieces of a puzzle and putting them together in just the right way, helped him to focus, sometimes even enough to sleep. He'd learned to cook by necessity, but come to appreciate it as an art after he'd returned from the Middle East, a little bit broken, wandering and disoriented. Cooking had directions.

The microwave beeped and he grabbed a dishrag to pull the hot mug out. The room smelled of rich chocolate and Dec smiled to himself. Yeah, he'd made a home for himself here, in these mountains, with his best friend turned brother all those years ago. He didn't want for anything, not the absent mother he'd spent so many years of his life waiting for. One day, he might not even want the woman who had pulled his still beating heart from his chest and squished it under her black stiletto heels.

"I've never seen anyone look so angry while eating a brownie before." She emerged from the shadows, shuffling until she was out of the hallway and standing just across the bar from him.

"I'm just thinking," he said, honestly surprised to see her. Not just because of the hour, which normal people were rarely ever awake for, but because he had caught only flashes of her in the days since she'd told them everything. She'd gone down to her research early the next day and he and Micah had been called out on a job not long after, arriving only very late the night before, after rescuing two hikers — one of whom had a smashed kneecap and couldn't climb out of a gulley. He also had the strange sense that she'd been hiding away, not the open, inviting woman she'd been in those early hours, but subdued and withdrawn. Which was why he was genuinely surprised to see her standing before him.

And a little interested, too. Because Lily Hollis had some damn fine legs. She wore only a pair of shorts, cotton and riding high on her thighs, and a Henley. A very tight Henley, because, though she was a slight, small-chested woman, her breasts strained against the V of the shirt, her nipples prominent against the fabric.

"Do brownies help you think?" she asked, settling down on one of the stools at the breakfast bar. Her smile was a little like a brownie, rich and warm and making Dec hungry.

"Do you want one?" he asked, his voice a shade gruffer than he would have liked it to be. Micah liked to tease him for being a real man about town, but Dec hadn't had a lover since Aubrey. He'd tried, once. After a rescue mission that hadn't ended as successfully as they had hoped — meaning it had been a downright goat fuck — he'd gone to the bar with the police team that had taken the lead on the missing persons case. One of the police officers, a young blonde woman named Katie, had been damn near as miserable as he was and, if it had been the Dec from BA, Before Aubrey, he wouldn't have wasted any time taking care of both their pathetic states, helping them forget, just for a little while.

But he hadn't been able to go through with it. He hadn't cared, not that night or any of the nights after.

Until right now. Until Lily Hollis stood in his kitchen in cotton shorts, with her peaked, tempting nipples, and he didn't just care. He *craved*.

"Let me try yours first," she said. "Ooh, ice cream!" A hint of her early enthusiasm was back, and Dec just watched her for a moment, as she snagged the ice cream container and his spoon right off the counter, popping off the lid and taking a bite.

She must have been doing it on purpose. If she hadn't, then Lily had been put on this earth to torment him, because Dec couldn't look away from her neck, from the way she wrapped her lips around that spoon and sucked on the ice cream the way he really wished she'd be sucking on something else. *Down, boy.* It was a damn good thing he was standing behind the counter, that was for sure.

"Ice cream goes better on brownies," he pointed out. He grabbed another spoon and cut into his brownie, bringing the dessert to her lips. God, she had beautiful lips. They were full and plump and a little dark and he could stand here and watch her eat brownies for the rest of his fool life.

She moaned at the taste of the dessert and Dec started counting backward from one hundred in a vain attempt to keep from growling, or doing something even stupider, like reaching across the counter and pulling her into his arms.

"You are a master cook," she said, when she had finished her bite. "I'm sorry that I haven't enjoyed much of your cooking while I've been here."

"Or much of my company," he pointed out. She flushed a little and darted her gaze down a fraction of an inch. "You've been avoiding me, Lily. I think you've been avoiding both of us."

There was a long beat of silence and she stood up off the chair and moved over to the tea kettle, busying her hands and not looking at him, though, of course, she was far closer, far more touchable than she had been on the other side of the island.

"Not really," she said, her voice far too bright.

"*Lily.*"

Satisfied with the tea kettle or otherwise fed up with her own pretense, she turned to face him. At this distance, he could see just how tall she was for a woman, willowy and petite, even though her head would brush the underside of his chin and he well cleared the six-foot mark. Good, he liked the idea of being able to tip his head down and…have her there.

Jesus *fuck*, what was wrong with him? Lily wasn't here for sex, and it was clear that being here, out in Montana, away from her shop and back in the field, was a big enough challenge, overwhelming and more intense than she'd expected, and he was standing there thinking about her nipples. No wonder Aubrey had played him so hard. He wasn't the kind of guy to buy a house and have kids with. Or the kind of guy to stick around for.

"Fine, yes, I've been avoiding you." She held his gaze. "And Micah, too. I'd go back to the ranch and stay with Madison, but it just makes the fieldwork so much easier if I can pop over any time during the day. Plus, she'd just hover and I don't want that, either. Sometimes she has a hard time remembering that her *little sister* is nearly twenty-seven."

Which was…younger than he'd realized. Of course, if Dec had taken ten seconds out of his fantasizing then he could have done the math pretty. But twenty-six… Jesus, he was almost thirty-four.

And living in a cabin in the woods with his best friend because clearly neither he nor Micah was a functioning adult.

"She's just worried about you," he said, pulling out the ingredients for another brownie even though she hadn't asked him to. "I know it's not my place, not by a long stretch, but I'm a little worried, too. You're good people, Lily, and Maddy — she's family. What you dealt with, the other night and all the rest of it, that's more than most people deal with. Ever."

Lily licked her lips, not quite meeting his gaze.

"It's not fair of me to ask you to just handle my breakdowns, though," she said. "I mean, it doesn't matter how comfortable I feel here, and I do feel comfortable, I don't know either of you guys very well and it's a lot to ask."

"It's not fair that you had to watch your fiancé die when you were twenty years old," Dec countered. "And fine, you're right. You don't know either of us very well. So get to know us better. Don't hide from us, Lily. We both know what it's like to hurt, Micah and I. We both get it."

A very sad, very small smile whispered across her lips.

"I hate the idea that either of you hurt," she said, her voice quiet. "And I want to, I do. I'm just… I'm scared, Dec. I'm a scientist and I've been compartmentalizing

Daniel and my job and my school for so long and now the data, well, everything has changed and I don't know... God, I feel like I barely know who I am. All because I got my ass out of San Francisco and stuck my hand in the dirt, real dirt, still attached to the ground and not in a flower pot."

"Don't think about it like that," he said. The microwave dinged and he opened the door, pulling out the hot brownie and placing it on the counter. "Just take one day at a time. One step at a time. Coming out here, finishing your research — it's a freaking lot all at once. I'm not surprised you were overwhelmed."

"Nicely phrased way of saying I had a nervous fucking breakdown," she said. "And it's not just that, it's also that you guys..." She shook her head. "Never mind. You're right. One battle at a time, right?"

He didn't push her. Instead, he scooped a large spoonful of ice cream onto the brownie and handed it to her.

"Only way to the other side is through," he replied, just watching her, as she dug into the dessert, intently focused and nodding slightly.

"Of course," she said. "I just... It was five years ago, ya know? I know you can't rush grief and healing, but part of me feels like I'm supposed to be over him by now, then I feel terribly guilty for thinking that way." She sighed. "Do you want to join in feelings-sharing time here? What happened to make you such an expert?"

"Well, when you phrase it that way, how can I say no?" he joked, but, of course, it wasn't a joke. Not yet, at least. Maybe in five or ten years... No, Dec couldn't ever see it being a joke.

"I fell in love and when I went to ask her to marry me, I met her husband." *Like pulling off a Band-Aid.*

Lily froze with the spoon still halfway to her mouth. "What the ever-loving fuck?" she barreled on, not stopping long enough for him to get a word in edgewise. "That no good... You just don't *do* something like that... I swear, I hope that woman never has children..."

"Three kids, too," Dec put in, perhaps unhelpfully. Definitely unhelpfully. Except the glint of passion and anger in her eyes, at his expense, was so potent and so beautiful that he actually found he didn't hit volcanic on the anger scale, like when he usually thought about that night in North Dakota.

"When did you find out?" She aggressively scooped more ice cream into her mouth. It was a little like watching a baby deer get angry, but Dec knew that there was serious fight inside her. God, she was still young and having gone through so much...

"March," he said. "Micah will say I haven't been taking it well, but I'm getting very used to the important people in my life not sticking around, so..." He hadn't meant to say that, any of that. Hell, the last thing he should have done was tell Lily about Aubrey. He shouldn't have opened up to her, as if she didn't have a thousand struggles of her own, as if she wasn't absolutely the wrong woman to be baring all his scars to, considering it was damn well set in stone that she was on a jet plane the second her research was completed — sooner, if it didn't go according to plan.

And, Jesus, shit, that's a real gut punch, isn't it?

Lily mistook the expression on his face and came to stand before him, running one work-roughened hand down his cheek.

"Your mom, then?" she asked, no trace of pity or sympathy in her eyes, just anger and sadness. So much sadness. Yes, her Daniel had left her, but it sounded to Dec as though he'd loved her to the very end. He couldn't say the same for dear old Sheila McCormick.

"I was ten." He turned, mostly to avoid looking into her all too discerning eyes, but also because her touch felt so good on his skin and he wanted more, wanted to feel the brush of his beard across her palm.

"She's a fool," Lily whispered. "They both are. Fools who didn't know what they had in front of them."

"You said it yourself—you barely know me," Dec said, turning to look into her eyes. "How can you possibly know that you wouldn't leave after knowing me long enough?"

"Oh, Dec…" She brushed his cheekbone and he closed his eyes, resisting the urge to pull her tight to his body, to feel her pressing against him, to give in to the desire to just tip his head slightly and… "I wouldn't leave," she said. "I'm not in any position to say that, but goddamn, those women hurt you because of who *they* are, not because of who *you* are. Anyone who can take care of a crying stranger having a nervous breakdown in his living room is good people, Dec. I mean that."

He pressed his palm over her hand, the one still stroking his cheek, and just held it there for a moment. A quiet, promising moment. A moment that got his blood stirring and thoughts of dear old Mom, even thoughts of Aubrey, seemed to fade, disappearing below the surface of the night, of them standing around the kitchen, like shadows against the sea.

"Lily." Her eyes blazed when he said her name, and *aw, fuck me sideways,* she had a look in them that made him burn, made him ache with curiosity and anticipation. "You've got to stop looking at me like that, honey. I'm afraid I'm not a very strong man."

"You're incredibly strong," she replied, but her voice was just a sliver away from breathy, and she clearly noticed. "I mean, you're capable and powerful and determined. You don't just bow down and take it."

Except she was wrong. He had bowed down and taken it — twice. The first time, he'd been ten. What the hell could he have done, followed her to the bar every night? Tracked her down? No, that had been case closed for a long time. And as for Aubrey, well, he'd found that the existence of a family had put quite a damper on the love he had thought he'd felt for her. The pain at her deception and betrayal hadn't abated at all, however.

"And what do you have to be strong about right now?" she asked. There was just a hint of uncertainty in her voice, an edge of trepidation as if, hell, she didn't know what was going on between them, either, only that there was very definitely *something*.

"You know damn well what." He tried to sound fierce, but, God, could a man sound fierce when looking at Lily Hollis with just a hint of wonder in her eyes, and something more, something that looked a whole hell of a lot like desire to him? "It's not a good idea, Lil. It's a really, really bad one, in fact."

"Okay," she sighed. "You're probably right. I'm hurting and you're hurting and this can't go well, not for any of us." She began to turn and, God, help him, he hated that he'd been the man to make her walk away. But before they got in too deep, before they made choices they wouldn't make if it were anything other than three in the morning and they were both standing in some real clothes, and not their excuses for pajamas.

"Lily."

"No, Dec. This is better. My being here is complicated enough to manage without forcing you to kiss me — "

He didn't stop to think, barely even breathed as he wrapped his arm around her waist and pulled her in, right in, settling her weight between his legs, as he held her tight to him.

"Does this feel like forcing?" he asked, pressing his hardness into her thigh. "Does this feel like I don't want you? Because, damn, honey, I have been hard for you since the minute you got here." And he was getting harder by the second, with the way her plush body seemed to accept him, right there, and the expression on her face when she looked up to meet his gaze. Her eyes held a certain wonder, smoky and anticipatory, and when she darted out her tongue to lick her full pink lips, Dec nearly groaned out loud. He'd been right, though — she was the perfect height for kissing.

She looked like she wanted to speak, maybe to convince him — or herself — not to give in to this heat, this tension that he couldn't deny had been building since that very first night. But Dec didn't give her the chance. Instead, he pulled her tight against his body, bent and kissed her.

It started out soft, just a brushing of lips that made him groan for the slow sweetness of it all. But then she was pushing back, pressing him against the counter, sliding her hands over his bare chest and...

"Lily." Her name was torn from his mouth on a groan and she moaned into his mouth. He slid his hands down her sides until he cupped her ass, soft and lush in his palms, and he couldn't keep from squeezing, which made her arch against him. Then her hands were moving lower, moving toward the ties at the top of his pajama bottoms, then...

Somehow, with the strength of a fucking army, Dec pulled back from her touch. He glanced down at her, seeing hooded eyes and swollen lips and... *Jesus fuck.*

"We should stop," he managed to whisper, his voice thick and heavy. "I want you to be really sure about what you want here." One glance into her eyes told him it was the right decision. *For now.* He wanted her and he planned to have her. But only when she was ready, and not a moment before. "I think you're still dealing with being out here. And there's no harm in going slow."

Lily laughed, low and a little sad. "You're right, of course," she murmured. "But, God, it just feels good to want someone again, you know?"

He did know, better than anyone. Sure, the reasons behind their broken hearts were different. Her fiancé had loved her right up until the very end and Dec couldn't be sure if Aubrey had ever loved him. But, God, to feel wanted and to want in return, *really* want — none of the half-hearted shit he'd been feeling these past months — it felt a little like coming home.

And that was a dangerous path to tread. Especially with this woman.

He brushed a kiss against her head. "It's still early. Why don't you get some sleep?" But even as she nodded and headed back down the hall, Dec had the feeling that he wasn't the only one in the house who was going to be up all night.

* * * *

The still-unnamed puppy whining in the kitchen woke Micah from a fitful sleep. Most of the time, Dec was the one who didn't sleep through the night, but ever since Lily had opened up to them three days earlier, Micah's mind had been a whirlwind of emotions, confusing and frustrating. When the camp wasn't in session, they could get called out on a mission at any moment—a lost hiker, a kid, a family—and Micah just couldn't afford any kind of distraction, not now, not ever.

But, of course, that didn't magically make the distraction go away and he'd been caught up in the images of her standing there, silent sobs racking her body as she tried to turn away from them. Then there was the way she had felt in his arms, her head resting on his shoulder, that served as even more of a complication of an already complicated situation.

Because he didn't just *want* her, though the fact that he did was all too clear when he'd woken up, hard as a rock, remembering her teasing expressions and the feel of her lush body. No, he didn't just *want* her, he *liked* her. He liked getting to know her, hearing about her life, about her daily research, when he could catch her for a moment. There was no doubt in Micah's mind she'd been avoiding both him and Dec since she'd first given over to the complicated emotions she'd been feeling about coming to Triple Diamond, and today he actually planned to do something about it.

Not that he deserved to do anything about anything. Lily Hollis was the pure kind of woman. She smiled honestly and nurtured plants, animals and humans alike and she made everyone in her life feel as though they were the person she wanted to see most that day. It was a remarkable skill and she was a remarkable person, one that Micah didn't feel all too keen on contrasting against his own baggage.

He picked the puppy off the floor and went to go stand near the window, looking out over the barely lit Black Reef Mountains and stroking the puppy's head.

"Did you get any sleep last night?" Dec padded into the living room and came to stand beside him. "Because insomnia seems to be going around."

Micah looked over at his friend, the man he'd come to consider a brother, in these past maddening years, and he knew in that instant that things were a hell of a lot more complicated than he'd even realized.

"I should tell you something," Micah said. He'd never been a man to mince words and it was still freaking early as hell. Without a cup of coffee in his system, he was barely a functioning person.

"Why do I feel like I already know what you're going to say?" Dec asked. Probably because he did. Dec was a master at hiding his own emotions, masking them behind humor and flirting, but after the way he'd grown up, reading the people around him was a natural skill.

"Lily." He even liked the way her name sounded on his tongue, found himself suddenly aching to hear her say his. Because she got to him. It wasn't a flirtation, it was deeper, richer than that. Nothing a hard fuck against a bar wall was going to solve, not even a dalliance or affair, like any of the women he'd been with in the past.

"Lily," Dec repeated. For a moment, they both just stood there, staring out at the mountain they had long since claimed as their own. Though, of course, it was more accurate to say that the mountain had claimed them. Between his heritage and his work as S&R in these mountains, Micah had no illusions about the mercy of nature.

"I have... I don't know, there's something..." *Eloquent this morning, Micah.* Not that he really needed to say anything, because Dec already knew and the reason he already knew was going to complicate this whole complicated mess a hell of a lot further.

"I do, too." *Ding ding ding.*

"So..." In truth, it was pretty amazing that they'd never come across this before. In nearly ten years of being friends, Micah and Dec had always gone their own ways in terms of women. And, of course, Dec had been mooning over Aubrey for months, in love with her for longer, licking his wounds for the better part of a year. As for himself, well, Micah had never got that far. He'd given up on the idea that he would ever have a family of his own a long time ago, right around when he'd given up on his family.

"So..." They stood there for a minute, just watching the dark sky fade to twilight, even the puppy surprisingly still in Micah's hold. Dec would talk for hours, but if anyone stopped to listen, they'd realize that it was never anything important. And Micah knew that he himself could be a stone without ever intending to be. Quiet and subdued had always worked better than anything else he'd ever tried.

"You don't think she'd go for Maddy's relationship, do you?" Dec asked, a trouble-filled smile crossing his face. He really looked ten years younger when he smiled.

"I don't know if I could," Micah replied. Not that he hadn't thought about it. Hell, ever since Maddy, Ryder and Christian had officially come out with their relationship, the idea had crossed Micah's mind, a little confused and a little voyeuristic, amazed and interested by something he couldn't understand. Hell, one relationship was hard enough to manage — how on earth could the unorthodox nature of theirs ever work for someone like him?

But four months had passed since Maddy had moved to her ranch from San Francisco and the three of them seemed happier than ever, if the amount of fucking they did in near-public locations was any indication. To his own surprise, heat flushed his skin, but Micah didn't analyze the reaction further.

"I don't know if I could, either," Dec replied, the smile fading. He turned back out to look at the mountain. "I mean, Ryder and Christian don't seem to have any problems, but I don't really *get* it, ya know? I don't know if I ever will."

"Right there with ya," Micah said. "So, with the exception of converting to polyamory..." He laughed. "Yeah, I'm definitely not gay."

Dec shot him a look. "You might be drunk, though," he said. "Obviously you're not gay?" He said it as if Micah had lost his damn mind, which, in fairness, was a definite possibility at the moment.

"I mean, right. But if I was gay..."

"I'm not sleeping with you."

Micah snorted, which woke up the sleeping puppy. Then Dec was laughing, too, until both of them stood there, shoulders shaking, laughing in the early morning sun.

"We have to let her decide," Micah said, when the amusement had died down and he was able to get in a word, a surprisingly concise and sensible word. "I mean, why don't we both pursue her and just see what she wants? Is that insane?" It felt a little insane, but not nearly as insane as not pursuing her, as leaving her to Dec, despite the fact that the man was his best friend in the world. Micah just couldn't ignore this pull Lily had on him and, though it scared him, he wasn't going to run from it. He wasn't sure he could.

"I don't think it's insane," Dec replied. "I think we'll see how she feels after a few days. But it's not a competition or anything. Nothing nasty."

"Nothing nasty," Micah agreed. "You're still my best friend, and we'll be together longer than any woman." Dec winced and Micah bit his lip on a groan. "Damn it, I'm sorry, man, I didn't mean to…"

"It's okay," Dec said. "This is… It's time for me."

That much was clear. And good. Dec had been wallowing and pissed at the world since March. What wasn't so clear was the reason that Micah felt it was time for himself, too, time for him to lay to rest some of those strict rules he'd followed so stringently, time for him to find some peace with choices he'd made long ago. Nothing had changed, not really. But it kind of sort of felt like everything had.

* * * *

Lily blew a strand of hair out of her eyes and sighed before tugging off her glove and throwing it to the ground with a wet *smack*. She pulled her clipboard over and jotted down a few of the vital details about soil temperature and pH levels, then sat back for a moment to look out over the mountain range.

For the first time in years, she was back to doing what she loved most, hands in the dirt, playing mad scientist with wild flowers, exploring their chemical makeups and the importance of the environment surrounding them. In the days since arriving, she had settled down at three different sites and was now on a steady loop of making rounds between them. The elevation differences and relation to the sun and the waterfall that cut through a nice chunk of the Black Reef Mountain range meant that she was actually getting unique and interesting readings that might help them to better understand why the common tansy, one of the most plentiful wild flowers in the region, was sometimes a helpful herb and sometimes incredibly toxic.

And yet, despite how much she loved digging in the dirt, she couldn't focus and couldn't find any peace. Not now. Not since last night.

Dec had kissed her. Or rather, she'd kissed him. She wasn't sure of the order of operations, only that she still felt the imprint of his lips on hers, still felt the warm, lingering touch of his tongue swiping against the seam of her mouth, before she'd opened, allowing him inside, making her wish he was inside her in more ways than one.

Which is insane.

She'd barely known this man four days and kissing him made her hot and needy and confused.

And guilty.

Because as much as she had desperately wanted to give in to the heat burgeoning between them—and Christ on a chocolate chip cookie, she had wanted to give in—Lily couldn't tear a small part of her brain away from the question of what Micah's lips might feel like on her own, how *he* might taste, strong and steady to Dec's charm and endurance. It wasn't *normal* to want to go around kissing two different men, not like this.

Then again, Lily had lost a sense of normal a long time ago and she found she didn't miss it all that much.

What she did miss was being sure of herself, and of whatever she felt for Dec and for Micah, because, despite her desperate need to ignore it, she obviously felt something for both of the men, an attraction, a desire, a depth, *something*. It was throwing her off balance. In fact, nothing in her life right now seemed to be in balance or sensible and she couldn't make head nor tail of it.

If a man kissed her, a man she really wanted to kiss her, she shouldn't start wondering how it would feel to kiss his best friend. *Right?*

Except Madison was a prime example of how it *might just work* to think about things with a fresh set of eyes, and if Lily had thought it completely fucking insane when she'd first heard of the unorthodox relationship Madison shared with her cowboys, well, maybe it had dropped down to completely freaking insane, and for more reasons than one. After all, who was even to say that Micah felt a hint of this thing between them? For all she knew, he was completely uninterested and she'd have to answer some pretty complicated questions about why it seemed to her like one man wasn't enough.

The better, more dangerous, more important question, however, was what if Micah *was* interested, what would she do then? Because she had to do *something*. She would be here at least another two weeks for research and, even if she did return to Triple Diamond and commuted to her research locations, there was no way she could avoid both men.

Before she could completely lose her sanity to this unanswerable question, crunching leaves caught her attention and she looked up to see the little golden retriever bounding up over the crest of the hill. The puppy skidded to a halt and fell face first into a pile of leaves, tripping over her limbs to stand up and rush over to Lily, where she then proceeded to lick every inch of skin she could get her little puppy tongue onto.

"Heel."

Oh, *my*. Lily had half a mind to take up the instruction herself, because when Micah spoke in that calm, authoritative tone, her breath caught and her heart pulsed and she had to swallow an inadvertent moan that threatened to escape. Oh, yeah, she couldn't deny her attraction to this man any more than she could deny the cuteness of the puppy now chewing on her box of pens.

"How about Penny?" she asked Micah, who was now standing over her. God, the man was large. His dark skin caught the afternoon sun and seemed to glow golden, like the leaves still clinging to the trees, and Lily had to focus on the puppy to keep from letting her mind wander to just how close she was to the zipper of his worn jeans and…

"I could deal with Penny," he said. "What do you think, girl?" The puppy proceeded to roll over onto her back and expose her belly, which made the great large man laugh and bend to give her a belly rub. Micah was such a series of contrasts, big and quiet and mysterious. Laughing, amused, full of love.

And wasn't there an idea…

"Penny, it is," Lily said, because she had to say *something*, anything to keep herself from looking into his dark brown eyes and leaning forward and… "Good name for a dog." At that, Penny turned around and looked up at her, a playful expression on her face, so

Lily grabbed a stick sitting near the foot of the tree and tossed it off a short distance. Penny was hot on its heels, grabbed it the second it hit the ground and she trotted back to them in triumph, her whole butt wagging with her tail.

"You are now her favorite person," Micah said, setting on the ground and wrapping his hands around his bent knees. Every part of the man was large — his legs, his shoulders, down to his big workman boots.

"She has good taste," Lily said with a teasing smile. She couldn't help herself. She just felt comfortable around him, like sinking into a favorite chair around the fireplace at the end of a long day. She felt comfortable around Dec, too, but it was different, soft breezes on a warm summer afternoon, a hammock in the sun. She needed to stop comparing the two men or she'd lose her damn mind.

"I'll say." Micah laughed. "You're my favorite person on the mountain, too." Something passed across his eyes and he shook his head, that long, beautiful mane of hair, now free in the afternoon breeze, falling over his eyes at the movement. "Which, of course, is a wildly inappropriate thing to say." His laugh was a little self-effacing, contrasting the powerful, confident man she had seen these past days, and she didn't like it, didn't like that he might think he was stepping out of line for something as simple as a passing thought. And one that had been rioting around in her mind for days.

"I wouldn't say wildly inappropriate," she said, tossing the stick for Penny again and watching the dog run down the hill to get it back. "Wildly inappropriate would be saying that you want to press me up against this tree and kiss me."

Christ on a...something. That had been more than wildly inappropriate. And also, what the fuck? She'd kissed Dec last night and Lily had never been the kind of person to go around kissing as many strangers as she could. But, of course, neither of these men was a stranger and just because she couldn't explain the odd and still somehow comforting connection she felt for both of them as individuals and the two of them together didn't suddenly mean that she didn't feel it.

"Wild Flower, indeed," Micah said, shaking his head. "You may look cute and innocent, but damn, that is way not the full picture."

She sat up and eyed him. "You think I'm cute?" she asked, because, damn it, she couldn't seem to keep her mouth from running a mile a fucking minute, not with him sitting there looking so sexy in those faded jeans and his flannel and fleece jacket. Part of her wanted to skip all the conversation and just pull on the open jacket flaps until he *was* kissing her against a tree. But she couldn't do that. The conversation was important. Maybe the conversation was more important than all the rest, because she needed some explanation for why she was so damn attracted to both of these men, despite not having taken a lover in years.

"Lily, you know damn well I think you're cute." He eyed her, a haze of desire in those deep brown eyes. "Not only cute, but tempting and enticing and dangerous. I think you're a whole lot of woman that I wouldn't mind getting to know better, if I'm being honest."

Whoa. That was a lot to take in.

"Really?" Because it somehow seemed a little insane that not only had she suddenly found her carnal desire after many, many years of squashing it down, but that she had found it for two men and that both of those men returned the feelings.

"Really," he said. He seemed to be taking extra care not to move any closer to her and she wasn't sure exactly why. Well, there was the whole *these feelings are complicated and oh yeah, I have a crush on your best friend, too. Crush,* like she was seventeen again and making moon eyes at the TA with the gorgeous smile. Which, of course, was exactly what she had done.

"I'm not…good at this part," he said after a moment. He picked up the stick she had been throwing to Penny and tossed it a short distance. The puppy chased after it, tripping over her own oversized paws and rolling over, floppy ears falling into her face. She found another stick and set about chewing it to shreds in the afternoon sunlight. Clouds were forming in the distance and the stark contrast between golden sunlight and ominous shadow caught her eye.

"Which part is that?" she asked, looking at him. His jaw slanted hard and ran straight and thick and, in a moment of insanity, Lily reached out and ran her finger down the line of it, feeling the stubble of a growing beard against her hand. Her skin, so pale and light, cut a contrast to the dark shade of his that wasn't ominous, not like the sky, but was fascinating. Enticing. *Tempting.*

He caught her hand in his and threaded their fingers together, his much larger one wrapping around her equally work-roughened fingers.

"The part where I tell you that I like you," he said. "That I *want* you. I do, Lily. Jesus Christ, do I want you."

She couldn't help it, her gaze darted to the front of his jeans, where, sure enough, they strained against his prominent arousal below. But he caught her staring and raised an eyebrow, some of the humor and amusement returning to his eyes.

"Yup, nothing but trouble," he murmured under his breath.

"I want you, too," she said, before he could stand up, before he could walk away and pretend he hadn't just dropped this giant bomb on her. But it was true, as she thought about the press of his muscled body against her back, as she thought about the feeling of his fingers on her cheek and the way that his smile lit something powerful and potent within her.

He still had his head turned away from her, so she whispered his name softly, "Micah." He turned, just a little, and she continued, "Why don't you think you're good at this part?" Because he was doing it all right, slowly seducing her whether he meant to or not, keeping her right at the edge of her seat on this crazy ride she'd been on for almost a week but had only just realized it.

"You don't really want me to go there," he said. God, this man was intense and wild and full of information below the surface.

"I really do," she said. "I want to know more about you, too, and you have to know I'm not just saying that."

His sigh was deep and rumbling, like the sound of thunder far off in the distance. A storm was definitely on the way.

"Abridged version, all right?" She nodded and he continued, "My family comes from the Blackfeet Nation. We're Siksika, Blackfoot, one of the oldest nations in the country." He sighed. "I loved my life there. I have two sisters, ya know, both older. Growing up, I couldn't imagine how anyone would ever leave. It was paradise to me as a child, lush and wild and full of the people I loved.

"When I was six years old, I got caught up in the river's current and dragged ten miles out of the reservation. I was terrified, Lily, convinced I was going to die, ashamed that I wasn't able to protect myself against the will of nature, even though I knew so much from my family. Anyway, an S&R team rescued me three days after I'd first left home. I had climbed to a cave and gotten stuck there after a storm. I almost starved to death and was too dehydrated to speak." He paused, eyebrows raised to the sky. "I knew that very night that I wanted to join their ranks, to use the skills my family had given me — skills I clearly had to hone — to help people and rescue lost kids.

"I didn't leave for the reason a lot of people leave," he continued, "poverty, the unemployment, lack of secondary education options. I left because I wanted to join an S&R team and I couldn't do that if I didn't."

"What about your family?"

He didn't respond, not in words, anyway. Instead, his face contorted into a fine line of grimace and sadness and he looked down the length of his legs at his boots. It was answer enough, to her question now and the one from before — *why don't you think you're good at this part?* Because he'd left his family to follow his dreams, left his heritage behind, left his whole life to do what he'd thought was right, and now, a decade later, he was still punishing himself for the choice.

"Anyway, I met Dec running S&R on a job in Helena, a little after he got stateside again," he said. "And he knew a thing or two about leaving and we became fast friends. When he first came up with the idea of forming the survival camp in the town where he'd grown up, well, I was along for the ride."

"But you never went back?"

His voice was filled with a sadness that Lily felt deep down to her bones. "I've been back, but that's not what you're asking," he said, his voice tinged with guilt. "I never intended to stay away this long. I always meant to go home. But then I realized that search and rescue, saving people and finding lost hikers and kids, maybe, just maybe, rescuing someone, that mattered to me. Teaching people how to protect themselves and others, it mattered to me. I couldn't live without helping people, and the deeper I got into it, with the dogs and the tracking and the business, all of it, the more it became part of me. So, no, I didn't go back, not permanently."

"Did they forgive you?" she asked him, even though she definitely knew, even though that pain in his voice resonated and gave her all the answers she didn't want.

"They didn't understand, not really. People talked about leaving the reservation a lot, but not many ever did. It's like stepping into a portal to another world and, when I left, I realized just how much harder going back would be. I got to see both my sisters get married, not long after I left, but I knew my mother kept wondering why I'd never be back for good, because at that point it was pretty clear that I had picked a direction and stuck to it, a direction they saw as rejecting everything about their culture and heritage."

He shook his head. "It wasn't, but I knew that I'd grown too far away from them to ever go back to life there, and they knew it, too. It was too late."

"You don't think you deserve love, do you, Micah? You don't think you deserve a family or people who care about you?"

He laughed, the sound hollow and sad. "I should have just kissed you when I had the chance." Despite the low sound of his voice, the words did something funny to her stomach and she placed her arm on his shoulder, leaning forward to do so.

"We don't have to talk about this," she said. "Not now, not if you don't want to." God, he was strong, corded muscles making his shoulders broad and powerful, and she had to resist the urge to squeeze them, like she really wanted to do.

"I think it's enough sharing for today," he said, a spark of humor lighting his eyes. "At least, enough sharing with words." Then, in a flash, he had scooped her into his arms and brought her back down into his lap. She seemed to end up in his lap a lot, not that she had any complaints about that.

"Micah," she squeaked and looked up to meet his eyes. "I don't think I'm the dangerous one here at all." She said that, because, God, he was strong and big and built and so incredibly handsome that her heart almost hurt, or it would have, if she'd been able to concentrate on anything other than the lust pulsing behind those dark, enticing eyes.

"Tell me not to," he said, "and I'll walk away and pretend that I don't want you, that I don't get hard the minute you walk into a room, that I don't find the dirt on your cheek sexy as hell. Tell me no, Lily."

But, God, she didn't want to tell him no. She wanted to tell him yes, yes, *yes*... So, she leaned her head up, tilted back ever so slightly, and parted her lips in invitation.

He took it, descending on her mouth with all the power and ferocity that had been sparking between them for days and it lit her from the inside out, making her moan deep into his mouth, making her want and ache, for more, for something, anything to help temper the insane desire burning within her. She moaned again and his cock pulsed hard against her leg. God, he felt big, almost too big, though, of course, Micah was a large man, and Lily's mind darted to the feeling of him inside her, of the depths of her ache for him.

He palmed her breast and she was just about to push him back onto the ground and set about getting rid of the rest of their clothing when his phone buzzed from deep inside his pocket.

"*Fuck.*" He managed to pull back from her and dug into his pocket, one arm still wrapped around her waist and holding her close to his erection. "Ellison." His face contorted as he took the call and resignation and regret passed across his handsome features. "We'll be there. I just have to grab Dec from the house, so fifteen minutes at the high end. Yeah, I'll bring Rosie and Axel. Okay." He hung up and sighed heavily.

"You have to go?"

Micah nodded. "God, you have no idea how much I wish I didn't." He smiled and helped them both to their feet, whistling for Penny who had been chewing her prized stick a little way away. She came bounding up the hill. "Don't forget that thought, okay?" he said. "We'll probably be back late, so just be safe. Cade called us in on a missing hiker, but he's worried about the storms and I think he might be right. If you lose power, start a fire and pull the candles out of the left drawer in the kitchen."

He was babbling. The powerful, confident, kiss-like-hell Micah Ellison was babbling. So she reached up and pulled the back of his head close until she was just an inch away from his delicious lips.

"Be safe," she whispered. "Both of you, come back safe." She brushed his lips ever so softly then turned, away from him, away from the temptation of kissing him again. When she glanced back over her shoulder, he was headed for the cabin, Penny at his heels.

Chapter Seven

Lily's phone rang and she pulled it out of her pocket and glanced down at the screen.

"Mads?"

"Which research site are you at right now?" her sister asked, in lieu of a greeting. Lily laughed and looked around.

"I'm at Site C," she said. "I'm assuming you're going to ask me to come down and visit you."

"Considering you're supposed to be visiting me in the first place," Maddy replied, her voice filled with amusement, "and not doing God knows what in that cabin with two of the hottest guys in Wolf Creek, then yes, I would like you to come visit me. Ryder says he just saw the guys out in their ATVs headed out to meet up with Cade for a potential search, but I can come up to you, if you're around?"

"*So* many things in that loaded statement," Lily said. "But fine, I'll be back at the cabin in a few." She packed up her research kit and headed to the house, taking her time. The Black Reef Mountain range was gorgeous in October — she had to assume it was gorgeous all year around — but the mountains were almost undulating in their autumn colors, with golds and reds reflecting the sparkling afternoon sun, sun that was fading in and out behind the clouds, as if the sky couldn't quite figure out whether or not it was going to storm.

Even if it did, it would be beautiful. This place, all this nature and fresh air and shimmering, clear water, it put her at ease, even more than Mia's reassuring words that the shop was doing just fine, almost more than just being back in her dear sister's presence, even if she hadn't seen Maddy in days. Not that she was doing God knew what with two of Wolf Creek's hottest men.

Except… Christ on a cream puff, she totally freaking was. How had she not even thought about this, the fact that, in the span of less than eight hours, she'd kissed both Dec and Micah, and liked it both times? The men kissed differently, which wasn't any surprise. The more she got to know them, the more she realized just how different they were, how neither of them was quite the man she saw on the surface, how they called to her, attracted her for different reasons.

Red fucking alert, Lils — you have to pick one.

She did. Have to pick one, that was. And yet, how could she, when both these tempting, striking heroes who ran off to save people who needed saving felt so right, their hands on her body, their lips on hers?

So this was what trouble felt like, then? Well, she'd certainly jumped back into the deep end of desiring a man with both feet. And with that thought, a healthy dose of guilt swamped her, making her suddenly cold in a way that had nothing to do with the gusts of wind blowing against the mountains. Every time she was able to go without thinking about Daniel, every time she found herself wanting Dec or Micah, the only two men she had actually wanted in years, wanted for real, instead of some perfunctory understanding of a famous actor's hotness level, she remembered why she was here, why it had taken so long to get here. And she still couldn't figure out which way was up when it came to feeling desire again. If it was so good for her to move away from Daniel's loss, then why on earth did she feel so damned guilty about it?

And, of course, none of that answered the pressing question of how she was going to pick one of the two, since her body ached for and demanded both of their touches and images of what she had seen Madison doing when she'd first arrived here, images of them all tangled up together, kept flitting across her mind.

"Okay, why do you look like you swallowed a lemon?" Maddy was already in the kitchen when Lily dropped her caked boots off on the mud mat and put her research kit on the counter. "I brought beer, if that helps any, some new apple-cinnamon blend from that family brewery that just opened up."

She reached for a drawer and grabbed the bottle opener on the first guess, all fluid, confident movements that made Lily long, just a little, for Maddy's simple understanding of her own self and abilities. Maddy never questioned anything. She'd gone to school, gotten a job, kicked ass and taken names.

"Lils?" Maddy handed her a beer then indicated the patio, where they both walked back out into the afternoon sunshine and settled into comfy chairs. She shot Lily a sly smile. "I was just kidding about the getting up to trouble up here. And don't let Ryder and

Christian know that I called the guys hot. They'll never forgive me." Maddy was...different, Lily decided. In the best way — relaxed, calm, happier than she'd ever seen her sister before.

"How do you do it?" Lily blurted out. Madison's beer was halfway to her lips and she paused, narrowing her eyes in confusion.

"Do what?" she asked after a long pause, her voice soft and without judgment, though concern colored the edges.

Lily rolled her eyes, frustrated with herself and her inability to put her finger on anything right now. Between the research and the sudden desire she felt for not one, but two men, her world had gone completely topsy-turvy and she barely knew which way was up.

"How do you always know the right thing to do?" Lily asked. "You're confident in all your choices and you never seem to wonder if you're doing the right thing. You just know. How do you do that?"

Maddy's smile was a little sad and she put her beer down before reaching over to squeeze Lily's hand.

"I don't know," she said. "I tried to plan everything out with the ranch, remember, selling it, moving back to San Francisco, the whole thing, and look at how well that turned out." She paused and looked out over the mountainside. "I almost left, you know? Ryder and Christian and I, we got into a fight, a bad one. I didn't think I could trust them and I tried to catch the first flight home. Thank God they stopped me before I walked away from the best thing to ever happen to me."

"You really believe in it," Lily said and, God, was that hope, pathetic and kindling in her voice? "How do you... I mean, how does it work, with three? It seems hard."

Maddy shrugged. "It's different. But every relationship has its challenges. Jesus, look at Joshua, that cheating ex of mine, if you want an example of how complicated things can be with just two people. So, yeah, it's hard, but it's definitely worth it." She turned and looked Lily in the eyes, her gaze far too discerning.

"What's this all about?" she asked. "You seem a little unnerved by something. Are you all right?"

At that moment, Penny scratched on the door to the patio and Lily took the opportunity of getting up to open the screen to answer Madison without looking her in the eye. The puppy bounded over and settled herself at Lily's feet.

"I kissed them." She said it softly, but when she turned around, Madison's eyebrows were buried in her hairline and her mouth was drawn into a tight line. Not a good sign.

"Any regrets?" she asked.

Lily shook her head. "I'm just... I'm confused. I'm here, back in the field, and for the first time since Daniel I actually want to share my bed with someone, but it's not just one someone — it's two."

"I'm not surprised you're confused," Madison said. "Each of those things on their own would be a lot to take in and you're dealing with all of them at once." She sighed and took Lily's hand and, for the first time in a long time, Lily actually felt like the younger sister she was, someone who needed guidance and maybe just a little handholding. She'd been keeping her head high, her shop running and her grief buried, but she was out of her comfort zone now and it felt like she might have a shot at seeing the light at the end of the tunnel as long as Maddy was by her side.

Just Maddy?

"I'm not going to tell you to move on from Daniel," Maddy said, her voice low. "I still miss my parents and they died almost twenty years ago. That's not how grief works. But if you do decide you're ready to let someone in, and if you do decide to let both of them in, you have to be open and you have to be honest, with them and yourself. This type of thing doesn't work without full communication. Trust me." She smiled. "You're not *going* to be okay, because you already *are* okay," she said. "You just need to start believing it."

Lily nodded. Madison's words made a certain kind of sense and maybe it wasn't the worst idea in the world to just see what happened here, to try to find some healing and peace in this slice of mountain paradise.

"Now, tell me about your research," Maddy said, changing the subject to something she knew that Lily couldn't help but chatter on about. "Have you discovered the cure for what ails us?"

"Menstrual cramps," Lily said on a laugh. "The tansy is good for menstrual cramps and pregnancy complications...if it doesn't kill you. And yes, I've come across some interesting discoveries in the soil analysis."

Maddy took a long drink from her beer and sighed. "I asked, so let's have it..."

Her sister left the cabin well after they'd heated up some frozen pizzas and finished the six-pack. The sun set early in October, and it had been pitch-black outside for the better part of an hour when the first crack of lightning streaked across the sky. Lily was settled into the comfy leather couch, flipping between HGTV and the news, when the thunder cut behind it, rolling through the sky and somehow seeming to echo in the vast mountains.

Dec and Micah were out there and, if the lightning and thunder were any sort of indication, they were about two minutes out from getting absolutely drenched. She tried not to worry over it, even as Penny crawled up onto the couch and buried her wet snout into Lily's lap, shaking and shivering in her arms. The puppy probably wasn't allowed anywhere near the couch on a good day, but she wasn't old enough yet to know that thunder and lightning weren't going to hurt her and if Lily was being honest, she liked Penny's warm, fuzzy touch.

Because she was the one who was worried. The guys were professionals. They scaled cliffs, crossed rivers, drove ATVs and rode horses through these mountains with alarming regularity. Hell, they taught other people how to survive. And they had Axel and Rosie with them. They were going to be just fine.

Lily wasn't so sure about herself. Carefully, she picked Penny up, stood and settled the dog back onto the couch. Then she grabbed another beer from the fridge before setting about making a fire in the grate. She was a little rusty, but the cabin's firewood stock was healthy and, when she'd gotten the flame well and truly crackling, she headed out to the patio and fetched more wood inside, enough to last a day or two, if the power were to go out, which seemed all too likely. She found a cooler in the far closet, large enough to fill with ice packs then stack to the brim with all the meats in the freezer, the cheeses, milk and yogurt in the fridge. It wasn't everything, but if—when—the power went out, it would keep a hell of a lot longer in the cooler than the fridge.

Then, while the electricity was still running, she rummaged through the kitchen drawers before she found a big box of candles in a cabinet under the sink. Psh, no tea lights for these guys, or the decorative wax candles she'd bought at the farmer's market. No, they were survivalists, clear and plain.

That didn't stop her from worrying, as the skies finally opened and sheets of rain began pouring down from the dark clouds covering the mountain range. She busied herself setting out the candles, trying not to jump at the cracks of lightning that illuminated the entire cabin, then the thunder pounding against the sky that followed it, echoed by Penny's soft whines. They were out there, both of them. And they were going to come back safe, damn it to hell. And when they did, *when,* not if, she was going to be honest and upfront with Dec and Micah.

She wanted them. Both of them. She wanted them with such fierceness that she couldn't think about anything else, except the way their hands might feel across her skin, the way their mouths, their fingers, their...

A shot of heat filled her belly, low and anticipatory, and she turned on the radio, hoping for some music to drown out her thoughts. Instead, all she got was weather reports, how dangerous the mountains were right now, how much rain they expected, how it might even get cold enough for snow. She shut the radio off and muted the television when another emergency report came on for the weather. Hadn't she left her iPad around here somewhere? That had music and no weather reports, nothing to remind her that Micah and Dec were out in the deluge and in real danger.

She plugged her music in and blasted her guilty pleasure. Though, of course, country music was only a guilty pleasure living in San Francisco. In Montana, it was pretty much the only music there was.

Miranda Lambert had just picked up when there was a shot of lightning then another, then one more in quick, almost violent succession. At first, Lily thought the sound that followed was thunder, but then she realized it was the creaking, groaning sound of the gigantic tree branch a little way down from the barn that was slowly, painstakingly slowly, beginning to break. She watched as it came free of the tree and smashed down hard against the half-dozen wires below, sending them careening to the ground in a tangled mess of splinters and dark rain.

Penny whined at the sound and Lily's heart patterned in the same desperate rhythm as the lights around the room flickered, seized and died, the radio, TV and refrigerator all zapping into complete silence. Shit. Order of operations. She needed to get the dogs out of the barn. There was nothing she could do about the horses—even the large cabin wasn't big enough for four grown horses—but the dogs, especially the puppies, were probably scared shitless. First light, then puppies. The fire was going strong in the grate and she walked around the rest of the room, lighting enough candles to give a warm, cozy glow.

It'd be a hell of a lot warmer and cozier if Micah and Dec were here.

But instead of worrying, she grabbed a handful of towels from the cabinet and arranged them on the kitchen floor, kissed Penny on the top of the head and pulled her dirty, muddy boots back on. In the closet, she found a windbreaker, Micah's considering how far it fell down on her body, but it would keep her dry enough. In a moment of brilliance — hey, every victory she could get — she grabbed the empty laundry basket from the floor. Bella, Allie and Jasper could walk back to the house, but she had five puppies to contend with.

She opened the back door and was immediately hit with a whip of fast, wet wind. The rain smacked her skin and she yanked the hood down over her head, then stepped out into the fray. The barn wasn't far from the house, usually less than a ten-minute walk, but every step was against the wind and it felt as though time slowed and the distance stretched endless before her. Still, she put one foot in front of the other, moving with slow and steady determination until the barn loomed in the distance, all the lights out and the windows rattling in the onslaught of wind and rain.

She'd gone one step at a time before, when Daniel had gotten sick, when she promised him she was never going to leave his side, no matter how the wind howled and the storm raged. And she hadn't, not once had she considered any other option than being with him.

But as Lily wretched the barn door open and it slammed shut behind her in the wind, the soft, damp scents of horse and puppy invading her senses, she knew she had reached safe haven in that storm. The daily onslaught of grief that had followed his death was no longer raging so incredibly strong — or rather, it wouldn't, if she allowed it to stop.

First, puppies. Jasper was pacing in his stall and Bella's fur was up in the back, the only signs of agitation in the two older dogs. Of course, they were search and rescue dogs and the Black Reef Mountain range got thunderstorms and snowstorms. This wasn't new to them. But Allie looked worried, the way only a mother, of any species, could, and she kept nudging the pups back into the middle of their stall, as if keeping them all in a wiggling pile before her was the only way they would be safe.

Lily grabbed a spare blanket from the stall's hay floor and tucked it into the laundry basket then looked Allie in the eye. Allie wouldn't attack, or rather, she had been trained not to from the time she was as young as her pups. But she was an agitated mother and worried about her young and Lily wanted her to know exactly how much she appreciated that.

"You're coming with us," she said to the dog. "We're going to the house, we'll be safe there." Slowly, carefully, she moved her hand out for Allie to sniff. Allie was tentative but soon bent her nose and, after a moment, nuzzled Lily's hand. Of course, Penny was in the house, she could probably smell Penny on Lily's hands, the scent not washed away by the rain.

Taking her advantage, Lily began to scoop the wiggling pups in the basket then tucked the blanket over the top. They'd still get wet, but at least this way they would be a little protected from the storm. Allie was already at her side when Lily stood and hoisted the basket onto her hip, double checking her hold, before she called to Jasper and Bella. They came in an instant then all four of them and the basket of puppies headed for the door.

Had the storm gotten worse in the five minutes she'd been inside the barn? The wind rattled at the windows and knocked the door back and forth against its hold.

"You guys ready?" The dogs looked like they wanted to respond and their company fortified her. Dec and

Micah were out in this rain with their dogs — she sure as shit could be, too. "To the house!"

They began a slow march back up the hill. Bella and Jasper ran ahead but never so far she couldn't see them and Allie remained at Lily's side, all but standing on two feet and picking the basket up herself. In a strange way, against the rain and the storm and the fear deep in her belly for the two men she found herself caring about more than she should, Lily felt honored by the dog's approval of her as Puppy Carrier.

Eventually they made it, pulling up against the back of the cabin, where Jasper and Bella sat waiting for them. Tree limbs were down all over the patio and one of the larger ones had fallen right beside Micah's truck, but she didn't spot any other immediate signs of damage.

It was difficult to get the door open with her hands full of puppies, but she did, and the whole lot of them stumbled into the kitchen before she slammed the door shut hard against the wind. They were wet, cold and still all a little shaken from the storm, but they were safe.

Bella and Jasper settled onto the towels on the kitchen floor, both falling asleep after she gave them a quick rubdown. She tried to rub Allie down too, but the dog wouldn't rest, sniffling and nuzzling at the basket until Lily began pulling the puppies out, drying them off and placing them on the ground, one by one.

Penny came over to join them, yipping and kissing at her siblings and mom, until they were all tired out and rolling around, yawning and stretching. Lily checked the food and water then closed up the kitchen grate — no point in six puppies running roughshod around the house. She pulled off the raincoat and hung it up to dry, then peeled off the muddy boots, her wet sweatshirt, soaked jeans and drenched socks.

Rather than going back to the room to grab more clothes, she stood in front of the fire, absorbing the heat. Shit, the power had been out an hour and already the temperature of the house was beginning to drop, more when the winds rattled the windows and cold air was sneaking in through every nook and cranny. Jesus Christ, she'd forgotten that her iPad was still playing music, the winds and whipping trees were so loud around the house, and she crossed the room to shut it off.

She was just about to give in to her panic about Dec and Micah. They would have called her if they weren't coming home, wouldn't they? Or maybe they had called the house phone, which was now about as useful as a parasol in the storm outside. But before she got the chance to feel truly nervous, she heard a sound, one that stood out over the madness of the raging wind, which meant it had to be either really loud or really close. If that wasn't their ATVs coming down the mountain, bears had started using internal combustion engines.

For need of something to do, in the weight of relief swamping over her, she lit a half-dozen more candles. Should she set the kettle on, make some food? She settled on grabbing towels and, at the last moment, the first aid kit from the hall closet, and was just returning to the living room when the door swung open and the two men stalked into the cabin. Before they managed to get the door shut, a crack of lightning slanted across the sky, illuminating them from behind, and making both Dec and Micah look rugged, powerful and completely freaking exhausted.

Then the door slammed shut with the force of the wind, sending the cabin back into relative silence.

Lily dropped everything and ran over to Dec and Micah, wrapping her arms around both of them and not giving a damn about how wet they were or the fact that she was standing there in just a long-sleeved shirt and her underwear.

"You scared the shit out of me," she said, her voice cracking just a little as relief rolled over her body at the physical proof that they were still alive, still totally okay.

"Shh, we're okay, honey," Dec said, using his free arm to push the hood down from his face. Micah did the same and she stepped back, a bit reluctantly, to let them take off their wet clothes and drop their gear to the floor. Axel and Rosie, who Lily hadn't seen come in, in her fear for the men, shook off at their feet and headed for the food and water bowls without much fuss.

"It seems like you did all right here," Micah said, dropping his soaked raincoat to the chair before starting on his boots. "Candles, fire, cooler *and* dogs? I'm impressed."

Lily smiled, her face stiff. "Penny was freaking out and I figured the other puppies would be, too. So I went down about ten minutes ago and grabbed them. Wasn't much hope for the horses."

Dec rolled his eyes, a smile on his bone-weary face as he unabashedly began stripping right there in the kitchen.

"I'll admit to being glad we didn't come home to a houseful of horses," he said, stopping only when he got down to his boxer briefs, which were also soaked, *not* that she was looking. Lily handed him a towel, which he used to dry his chest, shoulders and arms. The light in the kitchen was dim, with the fireplace partially blocked by the island, but she could make out the gorgeous cords of muscles and the power in each of his motions, as he twisted with the towel.

"I'm just happy you came home at all," she said, taking the towel out of his hands in a moment of madness and drying off his back. "What the hell happened out there?"

"Couple of elementary school kids on a field trip," Micah put in. He reached for a towel from the stack and shook out his long hair, wiping it down. "Four of them went off exploring and didn't come back. We found two before the storm hit."

Lily paused in her motions and looked up at him. "And the others?" She was almost afraid to ask.

"Injured, but alive," Dec replied, his voice low and full of emotion. "It's harder for the dogs in the rain, but Rosie caught their scent near the edge of the river and we followed it about a mile and a half before we found them in a gully. One had a broken arm and my guess is the other had a concussion, but they'll both be okay."

"Are you both okay?" she asked. "Hungry? Cold? I can put something together for you." And if that didn't have a ring of domesticity to it, Lily would eat the wet towel in her hand.

"I just want to sit around the fire," Micah said, tossing another wet towel to the floor, followed by his shirt. "And maybe enjoy the view with a little more light."

At that, Lily looked down, belatedly remembering that no, she hadn't ever gotten around to putting pants on after her own little jaunt in the storm. All at once, she was deeply, incredibly aware of both men's gazes on hers, of the way the candlelight cut across two hard, muscled chests, of her own complete lack of self-control, and she knew that if she had any hope of any of this moving forward, or keeping her sanity, they were going to need to have this conversation and they were going to need to have it now.

She sighed, because the last thing she wanted was to throw this at them, after they'd spent the night rescuing school kids in the wild mountains of Montana, but she needed to know. They *all* needed to know the score.

"Can we talk?"

Chapter Eight

Dec and Micah exchanged grim expressions and Dec unlocked the gate for the puppies, letting the three humans out of the kitchen and closing it behind them. A six-pack was sitting on the counter and Micah swiped it, dropping it down on the coffee table before the fire. He unscrewed one and handed it to her, passing another to Dec then grabbing one himself, setting down on the chair closest to her.

"I have...feelings." *Rip off the Band-Aid, Lils.* They were both watching her with such an intensity it was damned difficult to concentrate on anything other than the way their gazes made her feel, the heat climbing up her back, up her bare legs to the warm apex between her thighs—where she so craved their touch. "God, okay, this is complicated. I kissed both of you and...and I don't regret it. In fact, I want more. Of it... I mean, not it, just..."

Micah put his hand on hers adding to the heat she already felt from Dec's intense watch. "We know," he said, his voice barely loudly enough for her to hear over the roar of the storm. "We, well, it's not pretty, but we pretty much agreed to both pursue you, best man win, kind of deal."

She tossed her hands up in frustration and paced over the fire. "That's just the thing." She divided a gaze between the two of them. "It's not *either or*, it's *both and*. I want both of you equally and this coming from a woman who hasn't wanted anyone in over five years, so yeah, I'm a little confused."

Tension simmered in the room, and Dec held out his hand, pulling her into his lap. He was still damp from the storm, but his skin was warm and his gaze warmer.

"You haven't been with anyone since Daniel?" he asked, so much sympathy in his voice that it nearly broke her heart. But right now, right here, she didn't want Daniel. For the first time in so, so long, she just wanted to be Lily. And she wanted to be happy.

Still, they deserved to know the truth of it. "I tried. There were a couple guys I dated here and there, but I couldn't get over his loss, you know? It tied me down and made it impossible for me to open up, to anyone, physically or otherwise. So when I got here and found that I wasn't just attracted to one man for the first time, but two — well, that's what set me off the first night. It was too much all at once."

"And now?" Micah asked, angling his large body closer to where she sat on Dec's lap.

"And now all I can think about is how much I want to touch both of you, kiss both of you... God, there's so much I want. But I've known from the beginning that you're not into it the way Christian and Ryder are and I should have been more careful, so it's on me."

"Well, we don't exactly have a lot of experience with things like this," Dec admitted. His face was bathed in the glow of the fire, but she could still see a blush rising up his cheeks. It was amazing, that, how this powerful soldier, this *warrior*, was still able to blush. "I mean, we can try...I don't know, what if we tried dating, right?" He spoke faster, the more into the idea he became. "Right, you could date us separately, do whatever depraved things you want to do to us separately and stuff, just to try it, see how it goes, right?"

She looked at him then back to Micah' whose dark eyes betrayed none of what he was feeling.

"You're going back to California at the end of all this, right?" Micah asked, careful and controlled. "Just so we know the rules."

Slowly—and maybe it was slow because she felt a little hollow at the idea of returning home—Lily nodded.

"It'll be a release," she said. "An affair. Nothing permanent. We can agree on that. I mean, I don't know how Maddy is handling two boyfriends—one is more than enough, thank you very much." Even as she said it, Lily knew she was walking a precariously thin line to getting very accustomed to the two mountain men hotties in the woods company of the last few days.

"Speaking of handling," Dec murmured, his voice low and his body tense against her back—*God, this man's ripped*—"how's that all gonna work?"

Her breath hitched. She'd been worried about having this conversation, but now that they'd cleared the air and they were all safe in the cabin and doused in firelight, she was able to focus on the two, mostly naked, very sexy men just below and before her.

"Well, see, I thought about that." She tried to keep her voice steady, but Dec was trailing his fingers up and down her side and it was one hell of a distraction. "And I think that the only way this could work is if the first time is all together, ya know?" Her words wobbled just a little. Of course they did. She'd just told two hot-as-hell guys to give her a raunchy threesome. Even just the thought made her breasts tingle and her heart rate increase.

Dec throbbed just behind her ass and she nearly gasped aloud, trying for a deep breath and falling a mile off the mark. But, despite the physical reaction, she sensed his trepidation and when she looked over at Micah, he was watching his friend very closely.

"Is this going to be weird?" Micah asked, the words lingering a little too long. "Like, I won't lie, Lils, Dec and I, we're close, but not that close..."

She pursed her lips. Of course it was a lot to ask for the two best friends to just suddenly be okay with this, even though she'd known from the very beginning that it was going to be a hard-won victory.

"We don't have to do anything you guys don't want to do," she said after a moment. "It's not really fair of me to ask."

"We're not saying *no*." Dec almost cut her off. "But we just have to... I dunno, lay some ground rules. For one, if you're gonna compare cock sizes, you do it silently and to yourself, ya hear?"

Lily snorted. "What the hell?"

Dec just shrugged. "Don't you go denying that women compare cock sizes when everyone knows you do."

She rolled her eyes. "I can guarantee that neither of you have anything to worry about in the cock size department." Something in Micah's eyes flared when she spoke, and she knew there was actually some chance of this really happening. He was her hold out, Lily was certain. Dec, especially since he was sitting behind her, his very well-proportioned cock against her ass, would be the easier of the two to convince.

"Micah, do you have any rules?" If she kept the conversation going, she might just be able to get them over to the dark side.

Micah shook his head, wet hair catching against his cheek, but it was a motion of confusion and not denial.

"I don't know," he said after a moment. "It's just, sure I've seen Dec's bare ass, way more than I'd care for, but never in a sexual way. It's freaking me out a little, if you want the truth."

Before Lily could respond, not that she had much idea as to what to say, Dec piped up, "Don't lie, I know how you like it." He put on a high, falsetto voice. "I want you, I need you, *oh, baby, oh, baby*."

Lily turned around to face him, brows furrowed. "Did you just quote *10 Things I Hate About You?* Like Health Ledger, Julia Styles, *10 Things I Hate About You?*" *Can this night get any more bizarre?*

"I know you're not afraid of me, but you have thought about me naked." Dec waggled a brow and Lily just rolled her eyes.

"Obviously, I've thought about you naked," she said. "That's why we're having this conversation. I've thought about both of you naked and I've decided that I want to do more than just think about it." She paused. "I know it's a lot to ask. This isn't the kind of relationship you guys share and it's…I don't know, unfair. But I keep coming back to the idea of somehow choosing and that just seems impossible."

Something in Micah's eyes changed, and they grew somehow darker, more intense, a hint of the true power and mystery deep inside coming to the fore.

"You really feel that way?" he asked.

Lily nodded.

Dec kissed her shoulder, speaking quietly against her skin.

"That's a lot to take in, Lily," he said quietly, the depth and tone of his voice showing that he understood exactly how strongly she felt those words. "The way I see it, if the only way I'm going to touch you is with my best friend in the room, then all right."

Relief and hope zinged through her. This, somehow, some crazy way, might just have a chance of working.

But these waters were new and needed navigating, so instead of turning around and kissing him like she wanted to do, she looked over at Micah, waiting for his response. His eyes didn't hide anything anymore, but blazed, hot and demanding, and she knew for a fact that he was about to fulfill about ten of her top fantasies. And before she got the chance to say anything, to comment, maybe, on how she'd just made this all awkward as hell, Micah bent forward and captured her mouth.

Christ on a cactus, the man could fucking kiss. His touch was hot and demanding and not even a little of the soft sweetness she'd seen from him, both in kissing and otherwise. He wanted and she wanted to give him everything, wanted to tempt the beast and stoke the fire in his eyes. She moaned deep in her throat and rocked a little in Dec's lap, which made his cock harden even more against his briefs and her thin scrap of cotton panties.

"Whatever you just did, Micah," Dec said, his voice a low, growling noise, "do it again." He bent low and murmured into her ear, "Rock against me, honey. Feels so good when you do that." Given that her body burned with unspent desire that had been building essentially since the day she'd arrived, and the fact that she hadn't shared an orgasm with a man in years, Lily felt pretty goddamned good right now, too.

She pressed back, enjoying the way Dec responded to her so naturally, feeling the throb of his desire in time with her crazed heart, and she had to pull back from Micah's demanding kisses to collect herself.

"You all right?" Micah's voice was rough and low and Lily took no small amount of pride in being the one who made him sound that way.

"Hell, yeah, I'm all right," she said, eliciting a chuckle from both men. "I'm just a little overwhelmed, that's all."

"You're thinking too much," Dec murmured against her ear. "Why don't you let us do all the thinking for you?" And in one fell swoop, he had her pinned below him on the couch, legs spread wide and feet on the floor. She didn't need to look at either of them to enjoy the heated weight of their gazes and damn if that wasn't hot and heady enough to make her practically come right then and there.

"But first..." Dec's voice had a low chuckle to it, and Lily rolled her eyes before he even said a word. "I think we should lighten a little of the tension here." And without hesitating a second, he dropped his briefs to the ground. "Ass as bare as the day I was born." He waggled it a little and even Micah, who was trying so hard, bless him, couldn't keep his lips from twisting into a manic grin.

"Jesus Christ, McCormick," he said on a groan that was definitely a laugh. "Show her 'cause your pale ass just ain't doing it for me."

But they were laughing, and laughing was good because, just as Dec has intended, the tension in the room did let up a little, and some of the seriousness faded from Micah's face.

Then Dec was back at her level, sliding his hands up her shirt, teasing across her belly and making her squirm and arch into his touch.

"Does my bare ass do it for you, Lils?"

She wanted to laugh, but he tweaked a nipple and it came out as a groan.

"You know it does, you tease," she murmured. "Micah…"

It was his turn to laugh into a groan and he shook his head. "Greedy thing," he murmured. "You just want two naked men waiting on your every whim." Instead of stripping, like Dec, he slid down between her legs and her senses were shorting out because Dec had one hand wrapped around her breast and Micah was pressing heated kisses to the insides of her thighs.

"Fuck, so fucking good." Her words came out a scramble of demands and desires, but she couldn't stop them, couldn't stop herself, because she wanted more, *needed* more.

"Keep telling us what you want, Lily," Micah said, low and close to the skin right at the inside of her thigh. "It's hot as fuck when you talk dirty and I want to hear more."

And she didn't have to fake it. "Kiss my pussy." It came out more like a plea than a demand, but Micah didn't seem to mind, because he moved his mouth across the cotton of her panties and pressed a heated kiss to her center over the fabric. She arched and Dec just pinned her down with one hand on her hip.

"Easy there, cowgirl," he murmured. "The ride will be open all night long."

She tried to laugh, but it came out as a desperate groan, as Micah bent lower and lapped at her wet, hot pussy, growing wetter and needier with every caress of his tongue over the fabric. She ran her hand through those thick, long strands of his hair and pulled tight, eliciting a groan from the depths of his chest that sounded more animal than man.

"I want to see you," he demanded. Dec helped her sit up and peel the long-sleeved shirt off her body. It had felt so cool in the cabin before, when the heat had first started to drop after the power went out, but though she was nearly bare, Lily didn't feel anything but burning hot and ready to burst.

"Panties," Micah demanded. "Now." His intensity should have scared her, but instead it made her nipples pebble to hard peaks and she had to swallow hard.

"You like being told what to do, don't you, honey?" Dec asked, twisting his fingers around one of her nipples as Micah, clearly impatient of waiting for her to do it, pressed her legs together and pulled her panties down, tossing them off to the side.

"I do," Lily admitted. "It…turns me on."

"Say it," he murmured, his voice no longer filled with humor or false charm, but deep and carnal and needy as her own. "Tell us what it makes you feel."

"Wet." She struggled against the pleasure, bucking hard when Micah ran a finger down her slit and Dec held her in place. Then he stopped. Fine, she'd play their game. It certainly wouldn't be any kind of hardship. "It makes my pussy wet and my nipples swollen and...I want to feel filled."

Dec wrapped his hand around her cheek, sliding his fingers across her neck just enough to pinch, and the small bite of pain doubled all the insane pleasure.

"So sweet, so soft," he murmured, each word dripping hot with desire. "I bet you're going to feel amazing wrapped around my cock. I bet you'll come the second you get something inside you. Isn't that right?"

She tried to shake her head, because she needed to have some dignity through this whole thing, right, but then Micah slipped one finger between her folds and her breath caught in her chest and she froze, hovering right at the edge of her pleasure, until he slipped in another finger and began stroking and Lily felt that rising pressure and heat of her oncoming release and Dec reached out and plucked her nipple, *hard*, and Lily did come, right then and there, all over Micah's mouth and fingers. Her body exploded with pleasure, practically catching flame as she rode Micah's mouth, rocking back into Dec's throbbing cock with each new wave of lust that racked her body.

After a moment, she came down from her high, all too aware of the hard, throbbing dick pressed against her ass and the way that Micah's jeans strained where he was clearly so ready for her.

"So fucking sexy when you come," Dec muttered. "I wanna feel you around me the next time you lose control. Do you want that, honey? Tell us."

She was having a hard time thinking, let alone talking, but she managed to stand up on shaking feet, to grab the blanket beside her on the couch and spread it before the fire, just a few feet from the beautiful sparking light that would allow her to see both of these men in all their naked glory.

"Only naked people allowed on the blanket," she said with a laugh, before lying down on her belly and kicking her feet up in the air to watch them both. Dec popped up and was over to her in a breath and pressing kisses down the slope of her back. Writhing at his touch, she watched Micah slide the straining zipper down over his cock and push his jeans off his hips. His briefs were light gray, contrasting with his skin, and the outline of his hardness behind them.

"I want both of you," she murmured, more to herself than to them. "Micah, stop being a tease and get your fine ass over here."

He chuckled, but his cock throbbed behind his briefs. He came over to stand before her, just in front of the fire then he was sliding them down, too, down his flanks, down his ass and down, lastly, in the front. His dick jutted from a nest of dark curls, swollen and thick and slightly purple at the head, and she couldn't resist the urge to lean forward a little and lick the tip. The result was instantaneous and he put one large hand on the back of her head to keep her from doing it again.

"I've been watching you for nearly a week and it's been making me hard as a rock," he growled. "I'm not going to last long with your mouth on me, Wild Flower."

Good. She didn't want him to last long. She wanted to make both these men come undone just as they'd been doing to her all freaking week.

"I want to make you come." It just might have been the dirtiest thing she'd ever said in her entire life, but the expression in his eyes made her damn happy to have said it, especially when he brushed one rough finger across her lips, parting them and slipping the digit into her mouth. He tasted like fresh rain and the smell of fall, all rioting masculinity and silken sweetness and burning wild fires rolled into one, and she sucked hard on his finger, taking him into her mouth and rolling her tongue across him.

She could have sucked his finger and watched his expression all night, but Dec chose that moment to pull her kicked-up legs apart and press his mouth to the curve of her back, to the tops of her legs, around the edges of her ass until she was panting and sucking harder on Micah's finger and moaning against the dual sensations overwhelming her.

With a look of regret, Micah pulled his finger free from her mouth at the same time that Dec slid one finger inside her cunt, then another. She arched up off the blanket, his fingers large and intense in this position, and she wondered, needed to know, how he would feel driving into her.

"Dec…" His name came out on a groan and she couldn't even bother to be embarrassed because, *God damn*, that man had a thick, powerful cock and she ached to feel more than just the press of it against her leg when she whimpered.

"How do you want this to go, baby?" he ask, slowly, *fucking bastard*, sliding his fingers in and out of her folds. "Tell us and you know we'll give you what you want."

Wasn't that the God's honest truth?

"I want you to fuck me while I suck Micah's cock." Oh, she definitely got the dirty talk thing now. She'd never gotten it before, but the words rolled hot and demanding off her lips, "And I swear to God, if someone doesn't touch me soon, I'm getting back into the shower and taking care of it myself. Again."

That got a reaction out of Micah, who finally, thank *fuck,* slid down to his knees, his bulging hardness just a few inches away from her mouth now.

"You touched yourself in the shower?" he asked, voice more groan than speech. "Use your words, Lily, 'cause I want to know every fucking detail."

She had to admit, there was something to be said about quite literally bringing a man as powerful as a mountain to his knees. As she spoke, Dec stroked her pussy, sliding one more finger deep inside her, pulsing and moving with a rhythm that pushed her higher to the edge and kept her there, teasing, challenging, forcing her to hold on right at the precipice of pleasure.

"Showerhead..." she moaned. "Fuck, I sprayed my pussy with the showerhead." *Thinking about them. Thinking about* this.

"And did you touch your breasts?" Micah reached out and stroked one, pausing to flick her nipple, which made her clench the blanket in her fist.

"God, *yessss.* I played with my nipples and my clit and I had to bite my lip so you guys wouldn't hear me come."

Dec slapped her ass, not too hard, but it sent pleasure bouncing and ricocheting across her body. So close, so freaking, fucking close.

"Are you a screamer, baby? Are you gonna scream when you come?"

She shook her head, because it was almost true — she wasn't a screamer, not when she was alone in her apartment with her *personal massager* cranked up. In fact, the only time she'd even run abreast of screaming had been thinking about them in their shower with the water beating on her dripping cunt.

"I don't think you're telling the truth," Dec murmured. "Why don't we find out?" He reached his other hand under her body and, three fingers still stroking her throbbing, aching pussy, he pressed his work-roughened hands to her clit and pinched.

She screamed, of course, unraveling at the touch when brilliant, insane pleasure burst all around her, making her body bow and tremble with the total, complete intensity of it all. Her hands fisted the blanket and her scream died to a whimper, base and low, trembles still racking her body as the pleasure slowly began to recede.

"Fucking beautiful as hell." Micah's voice was a low, gravelly rush of words and she couldn't wait anymore, not for either of them. She wanted both of them inside her. Now. Which she put into so many words.

"Condom." She craned her neck to look at Dec. "Now." Dec slid his fingers from her body, making more heat rush through her, and she look up at Micah, still on his knees before her. His gaze was completely open, allowing her to see the depths of what he wanted, what he needed, and she felt a rush of a different sort of pleasure at the idea that he would be open with her, honest and vulnerable in a way she knew he was with only a handful of people.

"Lie down on your back," she told him, loving the way the fire's glow made his skin golden and earthen, loving how the storm still raging with some much intensity outside mirrored all that was going on between them right now. Micah did as he was told, positioning himself up on two elbows to look down his lean, muscled body at her, as she scooted up the length of him to kiss the insides of his powerful thighs. God, the man even tasted masculine and warm.

Then Dec was back behind her. He tossed a handful of condoms onto the coffee table beside their forgotten beers and slid one on in record time, before coming down to his knees behind her.

"Last chance to say no, honey," he gritted out from behind clenched teeth. *Not a snowball's chance in hell.* Lily turned to face him, her body curved and lit by the fire and small candles around the room.

"In me, please," she begged. And he slid deep inside her, just as she pressed her mouth down Micah's impressive length. Whoa, and there was the reminder of just how long it had been since her body had stretched to accommodate a man, let alone a man as large as Dec, because, *damn*, he was packing. But the stretch wasn't bad. In fact, the slight discomfort abated nearly as fast as it had come and she bowed, sliding up Micah's cock to take more of Dec's hardness inside her.

"Shit, Lils." Dec ran his fingers across her back, over her curves, cupping her ass with fierce hands. "You are so fucking tight, baby. God, you feel so good." Between Dec's words and the expression on Micah's face as he tilted his head back, eyes closed, mouth parted in sheer pleasure at the way her lips and tongue explored his length, Lily felt herself grow even wetter. God, was that possible? Clearly, because she was rocking back and forth now, taking first Dec then Micah and back again, in, out, each motion sending her higher, making her burn for that achingly near release.

"Let go, baby," Micah said. "God, I'm so close — please finish, I wanna come watching you come."

His words set off her release and the sight must have set off his, because he jerked, rough against her, and spilled hot and thick across her tongue and lips. As she roiled in the insane aftermath, Dec pumped one, twice, once more deep into her cunt then lost his control completely, flooding the condom inside her.

They collapsed, all three of them, the limbs and muscles holding them up in their weird little bridge losing all stability, and she fell forward, right onto Micah's lower belly, Dec's weight settling with a sweet gentleness on her back and ass.

Her breathing was ragged and rough, and it took a moment for her thoughts to fall into order. But when they did, only one important one came to the surface.

"When do we get to do that again?

The two men laughed, their distinct, spent sounds something she would have recognized a mile away.

"I'll be right back." Dec stood up and discarded the condom. When he returned a moment later, he had a handful of comforters and pillows tucked under his arm. "Let's sleep here tonight," he said, tossing them to the floor. Lily moved slowly, her body still adjusting to hot sex after so long, but a moment later she was snuggled warm before the fire, head on Micah's chest, with Dec pressed, a warm, big spoon behind her.

Her eyes began to droop shut, her body and mind both at complete peace and ease, and Lily fell asleep to the sound of breathing, easy and content from the two men beside her, as the storm raged outside.

Chapter Nine

Dec woke with a sore back, craned neck and the biggest hard-on he'd ever had in his life. It took a moment for awareness to flood all five of his senses, starting with touch — the hard floor under his back and side, the odd cranked angle of his head, the way his cock was pressed against lush, sweet female ass. Scent came next — Lily's hair, the wash of rain steady outside the windows, far calmer than it had been the night before, the clean scent of the fire, long dead in the grate. Taste was easy — morning breath, *ugh*. Sound was that same rain, mingling with Lily's soft breathing, in time to the rise and fall of her chest, pushing the comforter she had wrapped around her body. Because he'd opened his eyes and let himself feast upon the image, her lying there, sound asleep, hair spread in all directions, her skin so pale and contrasting his own permanently tan forearm, which she had wrapped around herself in the night.

She moved and he caught sight of a dance of skin and ink on her back. Interesting. Careful not to wake her, he slid the blanket down a little and... *Whoa,* good girl Lily Hollis had a tattoo. In their desperation and the low firelight of last night, he hadn't stopped to explore the way he wanted to, the way he planned to do today, and when he looked closer, he realized why he hadn't seen it before, in the dim light from the candles, in his need to be inside her more than anything else.

Despite running down the length of her entire spine, the tattoo was subtle, a single thin thread of a wild flower, a lily. It was beautiful, done in watercolor-style, weaving across her skin. Right around the edge of the petals, a few inches below her neck, was a date, and he recognized it in an instant. The day Daniel had died.

The thought should have sobered him, but it... didn't. Instead, Dec felt a fierce sense of longing and pride, longing for the woman who had suffered so many years alone, who had been so incredibly young while she helped to care for her ailing fiancé, and pride at just how well she had done, had lived a full and rich life, had come out on the other side, not unscathed, but certainly still breathing, still fighting.

If he'd had any illusions about this just being physical between them, at least where *he* was considered, they were shattered in an instant. Because he admired the shit out of the woman, slight, funny, wild as she was, with her soul running deep and her need to nurture and grow and love the things in her life, the people, the plants. It all made his defenses, the ones he had built so incredibly high after discovering the truth about Aubrey, sink a foot or two into the muddy ground.

But those feelings didn't make this any less complicated, especially since he wasn't the only one who had them, or the only one who'd had her last night.

He glanced over to her other side and was surprised to see the floor empty, Micah nowhere to be found. The phone he hadn't been sure survived the deluge the night before buzzed on the couch, and he managed to grab it without fully leaving Lily's side.

Cade needed a report after last night. Should be back mid-morning. Don't give Lils a good morning kiss for me.

Dec laughed and typed out a quick reply.

Thanks for taking the lead. And if she's willing, I'll give her a hell of a lot more than a kiss.

He could just imagine Micah's middle finger and rolled eyes and tossed the phone onto the couch before turning back to Lily. It was still early morning. There wouldn't be any sun, not today and not for a few days to come. The rains were still rolling in and up from both the west and south and there were several reports of more thunderstorms coming at the end of the week. Still, Dec's internal alarm clock was one punctual SOB and a quick glance at the clock on the mantel showed that he was only ten minutes off his guess. Six-thirteen.

Still, though she wouldn't be getting much research done today, Dec couldn't let Lily continue to sleep on the hardwood, much stupider idea than it had been last night, floor, and stroked her arm with deliberate slowness, kissing the side of her temple before murmuring in her ear.

"Time to get up, honey," he said. "We should at least get you into a real bed, if you want to sleep more."

She rolled over to look at him and Dec's heart seized a little. God, this woman was beautiful. She was sexy as hell, that much he had first-hand proof of, but she was also completely beautiful, especially when she looked at him with hazy, hooded eyes and mussed hair, her lips swollen and full from the events of the night before.

"Where's Micah?" she asked. Hmm, he'd expect that question to sting more, but part of him understood her need to keep things even, fair, at least in the beginning. He got it, mostly. Dec didn't think he'd be in any sort of similar situation anytime soon, so he just had to guess.

"Police station," he said, unable to stop touching her, watching her, running his hands up and down the length of her arm. "He'll be back in an hour or so, weather permitting, had to record the details of last night's rescue."

She nodded and slowly, groggily, came up to a seated position, massaging out her back.

"You know, I think I've officially hit the point in my adult life where I can't sleep on the floor anymore." She laughed. "I never thought twenty-six would feel so old."

Dec raised an eyebrow. "Now, I feel like I have one foot in the grave. You know I'm thirty-three, right?"

She winced. "I hope I look as good as you do when I hit thirty-three. Really, though, next time I think I'll sleep on the floor for shits and giggles, talk me out of it, would ya?"

He pulled her closer to him and turned her body, malleable in his hands, so that her back faced him. Then he began kneading out the kinks in her back and neck, enjoying every little breathy moan that escaped those delicious, swollen lips.

"You can cook, massage and make me come," she said on a laugh. "Let me guess, you kick puppies on the street? Steal parking spots from old ladies? There must be something wrong with you."

She turned to face him and Dec couldn't get enough of those gorgeous green eyes. Lily was like a garden, all earthen tones and fresh, natural beauty, her sun-streaked hair, her freckles, her dusty-rose smile.

"The only thing wrong with me is my lack of focus right now," he said. He slid his hands up and down her back. "It seems like no matter what I'm supposed to be paying attention to, I keep coming back to this image of you in the shower."

She let out a low laugh that could have been a moan. "And why is this bad?"

He was up and off the floor, creaky knees, night spent on the ground be damned, helping her to her feet in an instant.

"Let me wash your back," he murmured against her ear. "Let's steam up all the windows and get dirty while we get clean."

It was obvious that she was trying to keep the truth of just how much she wanted him, too, from coming across, but he felt it in the subtle arch of her back and the way her breath caught in her throat at his words.

"Well," she finally managed, "what you waiting for?" She took off down the hall and made for the bathroom, but Dec pulled her toward his room.

"I have something way better, not that I won't forever imagine you touching yourself in our shower, because you fucking know I will."

She shot him a smile made of pure mischief and he tugged her down the hall toward his room. The room had a magnificent view. His bed, never more inviting-looking than right now, was pushed up against a wall made entirely of one pane of glass that looked out over the mountain ridge.

"You'll get to look at that later," he promised, himself as much as her, because *fuck* if the idea of Lily Hollis in his bed didn't pretty much just push him off the edge. "First, shower." He pushed open the door, pleased at Lily's expression of surprise when the bathroom came into view.

It had been his second indulgence. The enormous pane of glass that allowed for an interrupted view over the woods had cost a pretty penny, too, but Lily was sighing in delight at the sight of tub and shower, and business was more than good enough to buy some windows and fancy plumbing. The tub was sunk deep into stone, surrounded on all three sides, with a rain showerhead on the far end, over a slight step in the tub, to accommodate his height. It was probably too much, but he'd grown up wondering when the water was going to come back on, if it did, and on the days they returned from nasty jobs, he wanted to relax the best way he saw fit.

Looking at Lily, he amended the statement. The second-best way he saw fit.

"You're going to make it real hard for me to leave this place," she said, her voice quiet, and though she was teasing, though she was talking about his freaking shower, the pang in Dec's chest made him all too aware of how hard it was going to be for him when she did. No matter how much practice he had in the way of women he'd thought he loved leaving, it never got any easier. And he didn't love Lily. He'd barely known her a week. Sure, he cared about her, felt something deep and powerful between them that he knew better than to analyze. *But love? No way.*

Instead of reliving the delightful memories of first his mother walking out, then finding Aubrey didn't mean all she'd said to him in the year they'd spent together, Dec busied himself with turning on the water, letting it warm the otherwise cold room. Of course, the power was going to be out until they could get an electric company up here to deal with the wires he and Micah had practically had to walk through last night on their way home, and the temperature in the cabin was dropping with every hour. If they needed to, as they'd done in the past, they could head on down the mountain to Triple Diamond and bunk there for a while, but Dec much preferred the plan of keeping Lily alone in his house for a good long time.

She dropped the blanket she'd been wrapped in on the floor and stepped into the warm shower, letting the water slosh over her hair and body. A soft moan escaped her swollen lips and Dec stood there for a moment, just watching, transfixed by the sight of her soft, willowy curves under the spray. She didn't have large breasts, but they were pointed and perky and the sight of them made his already throbbing dick even harder.

"Are you going to come join me, or did you want to watch the show?" A look of surprise crossed her face at the words and Dec had to laugh, though the sound came out ragged and rough and he knew that once he got in that shower, in the heated, steaming spray against the cool October chill, he was going to be lost to her. Probably for a good long time.

"You've gotten bold," he said, continuing to watch her for another long moment. "I like it."

She blushed, though it might have been the heat from the shower. Either way, he couldn't deny how much he liked the shade of pink on her usually pale skin.

"I like being bold, too," she said. "I feel more like myself than I have in a long time."

At that, Dec stepped over the lip of shower and joined her under the spray. He gently ran his hands down her arms before pressing a kiss to the back of her neck.

"Thank you for sharing it with me," he said. She arched to take more of his touch and he continued his slow exploration of her skin, all the parts he had rushed last night in his desperate need to be inside her.

"Thank you for making it easy." She placed her hands on the stone wall before her and arched her back just a little. He groaned. He couldn't help it, not when her body was so lithe and inviting and he knew just how decadent her heat felt all around him. Without a second thought, he dropped to his knees, spread her legs and pressed his mouth to her hot cunt.

"Fuck, Dec." Lily inhaled sharply and he grinned against her pussy, juices already flowing freely from between her parted folds. Oh, hell yeah, he could get used to this. He'd never tasted anything sweeter in his life and he continued to explore her, lick her, taste her until she was pounding one fist against the wall and murmuring his name in a string of curses and demands.

"Eat me, oh, God, *yes*." Her words came out tangled and harsh and he already knew just how close she was to her release and just how much he wanted to be the one to take her there. So he brought his hands around to her front and began teasing her clit, swollen and sensitive and over the sound of the rushing water he heard her sharp inhalation of breath. "Fuck, I'm going to…I'm going to…"

She burst against his mouth, exploding, screaming even louder than she had the night before and he continued to lap at her until her body stopped arching and bowing, until she finally managed to catch a breath, until she turned around to look at him, guiding him up to stand, to capture his lips with her own. The fact that she was tasting her own release on his mouth made Dec's cock ache and he pulled back a little.

"I want to do this right," he murmured, because, damn it, wasn't that the fucking truth? "I did promise you the bed, didn't I?"

Lily grinned, her eyes a little hooded and sleepy and it made something deep inside him pulse with pure, unadulterated male satisfaction.

"I'll wash your back if you wash mine," she said.

They would have gotten through the shower faster, except that Lily kept pulling him in for kisses against the cool stone wall and Dec was hopeless to resist them, giving in to her tempting charms every time she moved for him. Finally, though, they shut the water off and he wrapped her in a large towel, grabbing one for himself before he picked her straight up off the bathroom floor and carried her back into his bedroom. She let out a small squeak but wrapped her arms around his neck and kissed the droplets of warm water off his skin as he walked.

The rain beat heavily against the window, casting the room in cool grays and blues, sprinkled against a skyline of fall foliage. When he placed Lily down on the bed, her mischievous eyes looking up at him, even the view of the Black Reef Mountains paled in comparison to the naked woman lying before him.

"I want you." Her words were direct and simple. "I want to feel you inside me. I want to ride your body hard and fast. Dec. I want you."

Never let it be said that being bold was overrated.

"How do you want me, honey?" he asked. "I love hearing all those filthy words coming out of your mouth. Tell me what you want and you know I'll give it to you." He was pretty much terrified he'd already given her too much, but goddamn it, this was worth every minute of heartache he'd be up against down the line.

"Lie back against the pillows." Her words were no longer filled with amusement but instead spoke of a bold confidence that maybe turned him on even more. Dec did as she demanded then she was running down the length of his body, kissing his chest, his collarbones, his stomach, sliding up to kiss his lips, long and lingering and so decadent that there was no way he'd last long under her seductive assault. He buried his hands in her hair and ran them down her back and she shuddered under his touch before pulling away from him.

"Condoms?" Her voice was breathy and a little out of control. *Good.* He nodded to the drawer by the side of the bed.

"Top left."

She rolled off him, fucking pity, that, and opened the drawer. Her eyebrows rose and her expression changed. She tossed a condom onto the bed and held up a bottle of lube.

"Surely, the women you're with don't need any encouragement?"

Dec laughed, but his cheeks heated and embarrassment flushed up his body. Not embarrassment. He wasn't going to be embarrassed, not by this. After all, she had her proclivities, Ryder and Christian had theirs and Madison Hollis certainly wasn't going to win any Nun of the Year awards. Dec was entitled to a fantasy or two of his own.

"It's...it's not for the women," he managed. Her raised eyebrow indicated the question on her lips before she said it and he beat her to the punch. "Not gay, Lils, or bisexual or whatever." All right, this was going to be over faster if he just freaking said it, here. "It's for me. It feels good with fingers sometimes. But I'm not asking or anything."

She looked him square in the eye as she crawled back over across the bed, the bottle of lube still in her hand. The expression in her eyes was one of curiosity and...interest? Either way, he definitely didn't see judgment or reproach and so relaxed against the pillows.

"Do you want me to?" she asked, her voice a siren's call to his once again nearly painfully hard cock, standing straight up from his body. "Do you want me to ride you and..." She paused, trying to be delicate, if the expression in her eyes was any indication. "Use my fingers? I'll try it, if it'll turn you on."

Just the image of her riding him, one finger sliding in and out of his ass, was enough to make him almost lose it right then and there.

"You really don't have to—"

"I really want to."

She slipped down the edge of the bed, pausing above his cock and slowing. With all the teasing patience of a woman who'd already come and come hard, she licked down his whole length, brushing her mouth against his balls at the bottom. She did it again and Dec closed his eyes, pressing his head back against the pillows as he focused on the sensation of her mouth against his dick, the pleasure and pressure building hot inside him.

Then he felt the press of one cool, slippery finger at his ass and opened his eyes to look down at her, giving her one last, unspoken chance to back down. But there was determination in her eyes and she grinned one more last, mischievous grin at him before putting her mouth to the head of his cock. She pressed into him just as she slid down his length and every fucking thought fled, his body racked with pleasure, his mind blank.

She pressed and slid and rode his cock with her mouth, each motion pushing him higher and closer to the edge of her pleasure until Dec was sure he'd lose it, whatever pathetic grasp he still held on his control.

"Lily, baby, oh fuck, you gotta stop or I'm going to..."

She slid a second finger in to join the first and he did, careened right over the edge of pleasure when she hit him just *there*, her mouth still wrapped around his cock, her breasts pressing against his swollen balls and he pumped into her mouth, cursing and muttering as his release completely overtook him.

He lay there for a moment, his breathing heavy, mind blank and body still rioting in the aftermath of the pleasure she'd given him. Lily slowly slid out and out then came up the bed to kiss him, first his chest, then the underside of his jaw then brushing her swollen lips across his. She lit him to flame, this woman, made him want things Dec hadn't ever realized he would want again, made him ache to be inside her all the time.

"You're a goddess," he murmured against her still damp hair, smelling of him, his shampoo, his bedroom. The possessiveness that overwhelmed him in that moment made Dec feel a little crazed and he smiled at her with a wide, sleepy grin.

"I like making you feel good," she said, face somehow both innocent and mischievous at the same time. She shivered, and Dec realized that though his body temperature was raging, it was October in the mountains and the heat was out.

"Under the covers, you." He pulled the comforter back and hauled her cool body under the blanket with him and pressed against her back. "And I will never complain about you making me feel good." He paused and sighed. "You're the first person who I've ever told...about that, I mean. It doesn't usually just come up in conversation. So, thank you."

She turned around to kiss him, still somehow finding a way to press her lush ass against his dick, which had clearly not gotten the memo about having literally just orgasmed.

"Thank you for trusting me," she said, her voice quiet, as if she somehow knew exactly what it took for him to admit to what he wanted. And maybe she did, because despite having been in his life for just a few days, this woman had a way about her, something that just meant she always understood, always seemed to know.

"Thank you for trusting me, us, with being your first lover since Daniel." It felt important to say, important to acknowledge just how big a step she was making by sleeping with him. Both of them. Dec winced a little. He'd managed to forget that Lily wasn't there just for him, managed to remove any semblance of her burgeoning relationship with Micah from his mind. But that wasn't fair, either, and he tried to reconcile his jealousy with the fact that she was currently curled up in his arms, having just pretty much sucked the life out of him.

"Well, I did burst into tears my second night here," she said. "I owe you, both of you, a lot I think. But for now…" She rubbed a little harder and Dec had to wonder if this woman was a miracle worker, because she already had his cock responding to everything she asked for. It grew hot and hard against her ass and, by the time she reached for one of the condoms from the bedside table, he was already ready for her. Again.

And she was ready for him, which he could spend the rest of his life getting used to, because when he slid the condom on, then edged her wet opening, she spread her legs wide and took him, pressing back to get more of his cock inside her and wrapping her arms around his neck to pull him closer. He brought one hand around to her clit, stroking her, pushing her higher until her breathy moans made him surge inside her and she rocked, losing control, losing focus.

She broke apart, her pussy clenching around his cock from the inside out and Dec managed one more long, low thrust before he lost himself to the feel of her, to her heat and delicious warmth and the tightness of her cunt pulsing around his cock. He groaned hard and came, flooding the condom and jerking as he did, joining Lily in the aftermath of heavy breathing and glazed eyes.

"Oh, my God." Her voice was so low, so heated and spent that Dec's heart glowed a little with masculine pride. She turned to look up at him, hooded eyes glowing with her spent arousal, so sweet, so heart-stoppingly gorgeous.

"Between the shower and the way you do *that*," she said on a small laugh, "you're going to make it damn near impossible for me to return home at the end of my research."

Dec kissed her nose, all covered in soft, caramel freckles, and pulled her close to his body. And if he didn't mind the idea of Lily Hollis staying here, if he didn't mind the thought of keeping her in his bed, his shower, for a very long time, he wasn't going to think about it. *Right.*

Chapter Ten

Lily jumped when she heard the truck come up the drive. It was the second truck that had arrived the drive that day, the first being the electrical company, which had, miraculously, managed to get the power back up and running, so the house was no longer a frigid icebox. Still, she'd been so happily waiting for a truck that she'd been disappointed to find out they were getting power back and that it wasn't Micah coming home. *Crazy.*

But now it was. She recognized his blue truck through the windows as he crunched up the muddy, rocky path and pulled to a stop in front of the house and her heart hammered a little bit harder, all pretense of reading her book on the plants and animals of the Rocky Mountains completely forgotten.

This was absurd. Even the dogs, now just Rosie, Axel and Penny, the others having been relocated back to the barn, barely lifted an ear at Micah's approaching footsteps and yet, Lily sat there waiting for him with bated breath, wanting for him, too. She and Dec had fallen asleep some time earlier and she'd finally gotten up, gotten dressed and French-braided her hair, since she'd slept with it wet and spilling out in every direction. Then Dec had apologetically told her that he needed to do some paperwork for a new session of their camp and he'd kissed her hair before heading to the offices on the second floor of the loft.

She had tried to read, until a soft weight had settled on her feet and Lily looked down at the scrap of fur who had been her companion through the thunderstorm — the first part of the thunderstorm at least — and she resigned herself to some very difficult Lily-Penny playtime.

But she couldn't exactly bring a search and rescue dog back to her San Francisco apartment and she tried not to let herself fall in love with the little wild pup. That thought, which had come just around when she read the line, *One of the most valuable coniferous groves along the Rocky Mountains is located*...had been accompanied by the very alarming thought that she wasn't only going to struggle to keep from giving her heart to Penny. *Oh, no, oh so, so, so no. Because Christ on a coniferous grove, I am going back to California.*

Even though part of Lily's soul was drawn to these mountains, to the fresh air and expanse of trees and...and the men who lived in the wilderness, she was quickly falling in love with. *The wilderness. I'm falling in love with the wilderness.*

Micah came through the back door and his presence pulled her from that very dangerous train of thought. He stomped his boots on the mat, long, ink-black hair streaking wildly in the wind from the open door.

Behind his broad frame, she could tell that the rain had slowed, or maybe even stopped.

"Hi." Yeah, despite all desire to *play it cool*, which she hadn't had to do with Dec, since they'd woken up spooning, since Dec was so much more accessible, so much easier to read, she hadn't been able to stay on the couch for more than a second before crossing the room and coming up to him. Micah's grin was wide and not entirely innocent and though she'd come like gangbusters earlier that day, her body flooded with warmth and heat at the sight of him.

So instead of just lingering there, instead of making it weirder than it needed to be, she tilted up her head and kissed him.

Micah tasted like the wilds of the Montana mountains, like fresh air and fresh rain and autumn leaves covering the ground, and she wanted more of that wildness, needed it more than she needed her next breath.

"Well, hello to you, too," he said, his voice dark and rich as fire. "You sure are a sight for sore eyes, pretty thing." She felt pretty, when he looked at her like that, felt strong and confident and powerful and wanted, all from the simple expression in his eyes.

"I missed you. I've gotten very accustomed to sitting on your lap over the last few days."

He somehow made raising his eyebrow into about a dozen different promises and Lily blushed, despite the fact that she'd done a pretty big number on propriety the night before. And this morning.

"Well, my lap is a definitely available," he said, laughing. "You just might have to wiggle around a little to get comfortable." She couldn't help it. She glanced down to the seam of his jeans and, when she saw exactly how straining they were, she bit her lip, mostly to keep from allowing her whimper of desire to escape.

"Wild Flower." He had his hand on her chin, guiding it upward. "If you keep looking at me like that, we won't be able to claim we have the cleanest counters in the state anymore." She looked at the counter and Micah chuckled. Then his voice grew very serious and he boxed her in against the nearest one, his proximity making the blood in her body burn hot and her skin yearn for his touch. "Is that what you want? For me to fuck you on the counter? Or maybe I should just spread your legs and bury my face between your thighs. How does that sound?"

It sounded like the moan caught in her throat.

She lifted her head, turned to look at him, to kiss him, to tell him without words everything she wanted, when there was a knock at the door.

Micah sighed, very, very heavily, and pulled away from her to answer it. She could have sworn he was stomping across the room like a child.

"Joe." He opened the door for a man in a National Park Ranger uniform to step through. "Joe, this is Lily, Lily Hollis. She's Maddy Hollis' sister, here for a research fieldwork trip. Lily, Joe Delany. He runs the ranger program in the mountains." He walked over to the kitchen while the man named Joe, in his sixties, if she had to guess, with what was probably gray hair when dry, sat down before the fire. Micah grabbed a couple of beers from the fridge and motioned for Lily to follow him into the living room.

"I like you, Joe, a hell of a lot," Micah said, handing the other man a beer before giving one to Lily. "But I don't want the job. Dec won't even talk about it. You're barking up the wrong tree."

"You men know these mountains better than anyone," Joe said, after shaking Lily's hand and giving her a warm, friendly smile. "I know you don't want the version I offered you, but listen to this, okay? Start of the new year, we're getting a big grant from the state. They want to start a new research and environmental education program right here in the Black Reef Mountains. You're trackers — it's perfect."

Micah sighed. "It's not perfect. For one, I barely have my high school degree, and you know all the government jobs require at least a Bachelor's. Two, I don't want it. End of story, no more to talk about."

Joe sighed. "I know, Micah, I know. But just, just promise me you'll think about it, okay? This grant could mean really great things for this town, and I want to leave it in the hands of someone I trust — someone Wolf Creek trusts. It's my legacy, you know?"

Micah softened a little and held out his beer. Joe knocked his against it and gave him a long-suffering smile.

"You're good people, kid," Joe said. "Even if you are going to age me before my years." He turned to Lily. "You wouldn't happen to know anyone interested in running an environmental education program in the woods for the next ten years, would you?"

Joe stayed another thirty minutes and, though he talked about his family, shared a few stories of Micah's and Dec's troublesome ways when they'd first started working S&R, gave a good few bites of town gossip that made Micah roll his eyes, Lily barely heard any of it. Her mind had been whirling in dangerous, very tempting circles and she needed to get away from the idea that finding a home in Wolf Creek was a real possibility. Because it wasn't. This was all temporary.

This was all pretend, an escape, a way to finish her master's research and get the damn degree. Hell, this time in two weeks she'd be back at her shop and life would be back to normal.

Though, of course, what the hell does that even mean?

So, when Joe told them he needed to get back in time for dinner, she shook his hand and headed out to the back patio to get some air. The rain had stopped and the mountains smelled fresh and clean, as if all their sins had been washed away. She looked out over the ridge, enjoying the sparkle of gold and red and yellow leaves lining the whole far side, which absolutely didn't help her need to remind herself of all the reasons going home was the right choice. Because it was.

"He's a nice guy, but he doesn't always know when to drop it." Micah closed the sliding door behind him and came to stand at her side. Though the air was warmer than it had been the night before, she welcomed the heat of his presence, calming, solid and dependable at her side.

He looked down at her and something flashed across his eyes. Concern. Worry.

"You all right, Lils?" Realization dawned almost the moment the words were out of his mouth. "You need to take that job."

Well, shit on a stick, that doesn't make things any easier, does it?

"I can't, Micah." If her voice sounded a little sad, well, it was no wonder. She *was* a little sad.

"Why the hell not?" His voice was a different kind of rough, as though he was standing up for her, as if she needed standing up for, only the person he was fighting against was none other than Lily herself.

"You're qualified, you have family here and you'd totally love the job."

She peered out at the mountain intently, as if the landscape had suddenly, miraculously changed in the past five minutes she'd been watching it, which, of course, it hadn't.

"This is complicated, Micah," she said. After a long moment, she turned to look at him. He had his hair pulled back into a long ponytail and his features appeared even more defined in the low light from the arriving-just-to-set sun. "Finishing my research, leaving the shop—it's all mired in some guilt and grief I've never figured out a way to escape from. That's complicated enough all on its own. Let's not add in the fact that I'm fucking two best friends."

The words smacked the cool, autumn air and she hated how crude they sounded, hanging there, another thing to question, to feel a fresh wave of guilt over. Whatever was going on between her and Dec and her and Micah, it wasn't just fucking. Maybe she hadn't figured out what it *was* but there had to be some reason, some explanation for why she felt so intimate and comfortable around both of them, why each man was able to draw visceral, potent emotions from deep within her, no matter how long and hard she'd been pushing them down.

Lily sighed. "That's not fair, and it's not how I feel, so just forget that I said anything. The point is, that job is for someone else and I can't indulge the luxury of thinking about it. I'm just going to enjoy my time here and not worry about it."

She turned away from him and allowed herself to indulge in the luxury of Micah's big, warm, impossibly powerful body as he came up behind her and wrapped his arms around her waist. His weight was a comfort against her back, and then it was something else entirely, when he bent to whisper low into her ear.

"This conversation isn't over, Wild Flower. But I'd much rather help you enjoy your time here at the moment." He shifted just a little and pressed his erection against her ass. Oh, yeah, Micah was hung. Even through the layers of jeans and flannel, she could feel his hard outline and she wanted him, ached for him.

"That sounds really nice," Lily managed, but her voice came out this side of husky. She didn't have the time to think on it, though, because Micah's hand came around to cup one of her breasts, brushing her aching, swollen nipple through her shirt and bra. She arched into his touch, straining for more, needing more of his large body on hers.

"You wanna know what I spent the day thinking?" he asked, one hand on her hip, the other strong and powerful at the base of her jaw, but never too rough and never too hard, right on the edge of pain and pleasure. Lily managed to nod, despite his grasp. "I was at the police station all day, filling out the paperwork for last night's rescue, and, baby, all I could think about was you, touching you last night, the way your mouth felt wrapped around my cock, how delicious and tight you would feel when I got home."

Micah let out a ragged laugh. "I bet half that police station thinks I get a hard-on from doing paperwork because I could not stop imagining you, spread wide and…" He took a step back. "Well, looking a little like this, actually."

Instinctively, she spread her legs just a little bit wider, a carnal part of herself enjoying his moan of approval.

"Just like that." He slid his hand over the curve of her ass, cupping it with a rough motion and pressing his hardness into her flesh. "I love how responsive you are. Hell, I could probably get off just listening to you moan." With one large hand, he turned her head, tilting her chin so that Lily could look him in the eyes. He brushed his thumb over her lips then slid it into her mouth. Lily never took her eyes off him as she sucked and tasted his thumb, never stopped licking or kissing, especially not when his Adam's apple bobbed and his eyes went dark and hooded.

"Yeah, I could definitely get off to you moaning, especially when you're sucking me." This, of course, only made her moan harder. "I want you, Lily. I can't stop wanting you."

She pulled free from his finger and swallowed hard. "I want you, too," she managed. "And I don't know why we're wasting so much time." His gaze was dark and hooded, but his eyebrows went up in curiosity.

"Tell me, Lily," Micah began and, somehow, she felt as though he was walking closer to her, like he wasn't already standing there, right there, towering and powerful and huge as a mountain. "Have you ever made love outside?" The breath caught in her throat and she swallowed again before shaking her head. It was insane, it was base and depraved. And yet, the second the words had hit the air, her nipples pebbled and her pussy ran wet and hot with need. Yeah, just because the idea was totally cracked didn't mean she wasn't onboard—her body at least. *Make love.*

"What if someone finds us?" The protest was more because she felt like she should, because she was pressed against the railing looking up at Micah Ellison and wondering what it would be like to have him fill her right here and right now as she looked out over the Black Reef Mountains.

"No one will find us." There was an unspoken, *except Dec*, who was still upstairs in the office, but that was okay. They were all okay with this and if Dec did stumble down any time soon, well, she hoped he'd just leave them to it.

"And if they do, though?" Lily asked.

Micah pulled her close. "Let them watch," he said. He followed her gaze. "Oh, you would, wouldn't you? You'd let some hiker or rancher standing down there watch me fill your cunt with my cock. Tell me, Lily. Tell me you want this."

He was losing control and, fuck, if Micah — powerful, calm, easy-going Micah — losing control wasn't sexy as sin. Her pussy clenched and she sucked in a breath against the wash of needy pleasure.

"I want it," she demanded. "God, Micah, now." His fingers were already on the fly of her jeans and he was yanking them and her panties down past the curve of her ass. There was a bite in the air and he didn't push them any lower, limiting her movement, making her feel vulnerable and all too excited about what he was going to do next. She heard the rustle of his jeans and zipper and the telltale tearing of a condom wrapper. Micah's movements were jerky and needy behind her. Then he was there, big and hard and throbbing against her entrance.

He teased her, sliding the head of his cock between her slippery, needy folds, and Lily gasped and grabbed the banister tightly. Micah pulled her back just enough to spread her legs as far as they would go with the pants still on. "Hold onto the railing," he said. "I wanna see you coming apart, all over my fingers. I want to taste you, baby, feel you shuddering around me." He was there, inching his thick cock into her body. Oh, Jesus, he was big and hard as stone and sinking into her a little bit at a time.

Micah paused and slid his hand up into her hair and Lily pulsed hard at the rough line of pain and pleasure.

"You okay, baby?" he asked. "Can you take more?"

There's more?

But she nodded and spread wider, accepting the last few, thick inches of him until he bottomed out, balls slapping against her ass, her body expanding to accommodate his overwhelming length and girth. She sighed, feeling full and content and practically ready to burst at a moment's notice.

"God, Micah, please move…" Her voice was so strained, so desperate and wanton and she didn't wait for him to respond, just pressed her body back, riding his cock, taking him all the way inside her and pulling free with torturous slowness.

"Shh, baby. It's okay to give up control. Let me make you feel good." He towered over her, pinning her body against the railing, and Lily just gave over to the intense, overwhelming madness of his body against hers, his cock buried so incredibly deep inside her. Micah brought his rough hands around to stroke her breast, moving down her body, down her stomach and chest, before burying deep in the heat between her legs. He slid his fingers over her swollen clit and Lily was so close to the fire that she burst, disintegrating into flame and pleasure, riding him hard and losing herself to delicious sensations racking her body.

Her hands clenched tight around the banister and it took her a moment to realize that Micah was still very capably standing above her, clearly not having lost control at all. His body rocked hard, his cock throbbing, and Lily let out a shaky breath when he groaned against her ear.

"Again, Lily." His words were rough and hot. "I want to feel you coming around my cock again."

Her body was already so close to the edge, swollen and hot to the touch, but she knew she would come again and soon, if he kept up that rhythm of his hand on her breast and on her clit and his cock buried so deep inside her.

"Now, baby."

She did. The orgasm was smaller, but just as intense, as pleasure racked her already abused body, sending her into a tailspin of lights and need and the ground fell out from under her feet and she almost lost her balance. Micah caught her — of course he did, he was making it all too clear that he would always be around to catch her — and when he wrapped his arm around her waist, Lily realized in amazement that he was still inside her, hard and moving teasingly slow. It only took a moment for her to understand what that meant.

"I can't," she moaned. "God, it's too much."

He tilted her head up and she peered into those intense eyes. "Yes you can," he said. "And you will, for me." Goddamn it, he was probably right. Especially since the feeling of his large hands on her ass made her pussy somehow squeeze tighter with need and her breasts still felt swollen with unspent pleasures. His hand rounded the curve of her ass cheek and, without warning, he smacked her there.

Lily moaned, a harsh, guttural sound torn from the back of her throat. She'd never really played around with the whole spanking thing before, but fuck if the thin line of pleasure and pain hadn't just blurred, hadn't just sent her mind reeling and every single one of her reasons why she *couldn't* fleeing her mind. He did it again, a little bit harder this time, and it pushed her just a little bit closer to that insane third release she was sure would just shatter her. Micah smacked her ass one more time, growling in her ear about how she *was so fucking tight, felt so fucking good wrapped around his cock* and they were both breaking free, together, hard and fast and chaotic and wild, and Lily lost her feet, then they were both slumped over the railing, breathing heavy, pleasure overtaking them.

The sun was nearly down behind the mountains now, casting the whole patio and cabin in a golden, glowing light that made the smug, hooded expression on Micah's face all the more decadent. He grinned down at her, his face easing, the lines that so often crossed his forehead disappearing when he did. She liked the version of Micah most — comfortable, happy.

"I think I might be dead," she said, laughing even as the words spilled from her mouth. "Am I dead?"

He helped her to her feet from the uncomfortable position she had somehow slid into, helped her tug her clothes back into place before buckling up his jeans and readjusting his jacket.

"If you're dead, I'm right there alongside you," he said. "I'm starving." He didn't give her the chance to follow, just picked her up and carried her through the doorway to the house and into the kitchen.

Dec was inside, wearing that same sexy apron she'd caught him in a few nights earlier, the night they'd first kissed, before all this madness had begun. Before Micah even put her down, Dec leaned up and kissed her, squared on the mouth, right there. Oh yeah, she could definitely get used to this.

"You two are going to attract wolves with all that howling," he said on a laugh, which betrayed just how long he'd been thinking of the witty insult. Micah placed her down on a bar stool and grabbed a few beers from the fridge, passing them around. He was relaxed, his movements calm, his face at ease.

"You know it's not mating season," he countered, cool as anything.

Dec didn't fare so well, bursting into laughter before he managed to say, "It's *definitely* mating season."

Lily couldn't help it. She laughed. This, whatever temporary madness this was, with her somehow sleeping with and kind of sort of dating both Dec and Micah, it was working. Somehow, some way, they'd found a thing that worked for them. For now.

And she was only going to worry about for now. She was only going to think about how hot Dec looked in his *kiss the cook* apron and tight T-shirt, only going to feel relief and calm at the fact that they both seemed *okay* with this weird and unusual arrangement. Because if she went any further, if she thought about that job that had freaked her out so much before, if she thought about how Madison was here, if she thought about how freaking easy it could be for her to make a life for herself in Wolf Creek, Montana, Lily might actually start to believe it was possible.

She'd had enough hardship and grief and heartache in her life, thank you very much. Now, she had two hot men and a delicious dinner waiting for her and there was no sense in ruining it. Right, live for the moment. She could do that, especially when the moment looked at her with two sets of dangerous, seductive eyes, and all other thoughts and worries and fears quietly, easily, just disappeared.

Chapter Eleven

"Maddy invited us to dinner."

Her boots were caked with dirt and she tried to push them off by the heels but almost fell on her ass. Instead, Lily sat down on the mudroom floor and tugged at them, cracking the dried mud on her socks and ankle. The right one came off, along with half a mountain of dirt and she sighed before yanking on the other one. She'd always been the dirtiest one on her research teams. Back when she'd first started her master's program, she had marveled at the way her fellow researchers maintained their hair and kept their fingernails clean. For a while, she'd actually cared, too.

"Did she really?" Micah came into the doorway, the notebook she'd come to recognize as the one he used for his training program ideas in hand and a smug, knowing expression on his face. As she yanked on her other shoe, practically adhering to her body with dried mud and dirt, his grin grew wider.

"Fine…" Lily gritted her teeth and the shoe came free, sailing across the mudroom and hitting the dark wall at the far end in a cloud of dirt and dust. She sighed. "No, she didn't invite us, she threatened me with dismemberment if I didn't come down to dinner with them tonight then added that I could bring my cabana boys before making a terrible pun to the effect of 'cabin-bana boys'."

"I heard cabana boys," Dec popped his head around the door, too, and made a face. "Did you leave any dirt in the woods? We need some for our classes, ya know."

Lily stuck her tongue out at him. "We're going down to the ranch for dinner," she said. "I'm putting you on baking duty."

Dec rolled his eyes. "I can make a brownie in the microwave," he said. "I can't *bake*." Of course not. Because survival expert soldiers who lived in the wilderness would never bake.

"Then make a dozen brownies in the microwave," she said with a smile. "I'm putting myself on shower duty." She shrugged a little and the thick layer of dirt that had caked across her sweatshirt broke in puffs of dust and she grimaced. "I smell like manure." She yanked the sweatshirt up over her head and tossed it to the mat, before pulling off each sock and her disgusting, once black and now greenish brown leggings that had pretty much stuck permanently to her skin. All the while, she felt Dec's and Micah's tracking gazes, hot and admiring and amused.

"I've led men into the forest for a week and they've come back with less dirt on them than you do," Dec said, shaking his head. "Are you at least making progress?"

Lily sparked. "I am, actually. I've been checking toxicity levels in the soil at various depths, as well as seeking out the water sources for each of the three research locations, where growth is the thickest, and I've gotten some really interesting results. There's a pretty clear discrepancy between two of the sites, and I can't wait to get my results back to the lab."

Which is going to happen when I get home. In one week. She had one week left here in Wolf Creek and her fantasy nature adventure would come to a screeching halt. No more dirt, no more sexy mountain men. Just other people's wedding decorations and an empty bed.

But she still had a week here and she was going to enjoy every second of it she could, so she stood up from the mudroom floor, dusted herself off—that was a laugh—and strode for the bathroom. Dec's bathroom, to be precise, since she'd fallen totally in love with the tub and wanted a good soak before they had to go to Maddy's.

She paused in the doorway. "You know, you guys haven't shown me the full survival course. I saw the main camp grounds, but not the other stuff."

Black Reef Survival Camp was one of the hardest outdoor survival programs in the country and the founders were standing before her now, Penny wiggling around at their feet, Rosie and Axel staring up at them in full adoration, Dec complaining about not knowing how to bake.

"If we leave early, we can show you the Hut," Micah said. "We're actually thinking of tearing it down this year, but we might use it for one more program with snowfall."

"I'd like that," Lily said. "I want to know more about your program, since it's rated the second-best one in the freaking country and you guys are all tight-lipped and shit."

"That's why we're the second best in the country," Micah replied with a grin. "But we might be convinced to show you."

"Damn straight. Now, I'm taking a quick bath—alone. I'm filthy and sweaty. We can go once I'm out..."

Dec muttered something about microwave brownies, but Lily just pecked him on the cheek. God, even that, even the feel of his scruffy skin, somehow managed to make her blood burn.

She turned and brushed Micah's cheek, too, then headed for the bathroom. It had been a week of this delicious, sinful game and, the more time she spent in their presence, the more she realized just how little control she had around either of the men. The sheer power and masculinity when they were standing next to each other? It was enough to knock a girl on her ass. So, Lily kept to her mission. Clean first. The rest? Well, she still had a week, didn't she?

In the end, Dec managed to pull together a pan of M&M brownies in less time than it took her to shower and change into a fresh pair of jeans and a soft, cozy sweater. The temperatures had been wavering since the storm the week before, and according to all weather reports, that deluge had been the first of several on a cold front coming down from the north. She had taken the time to blow dry her hair, because after a day spent up to her knees in cold, very wet dirt, she wanted to indulge in a little feminine R & R, though Lily had no doubt that there was more than a little R & R available whenever she wanted.

This was...too easy. Even the air of awkwardness that she'd expected to linger whenever she touched Micah or Dec in front of the other hadn't hit full capacity, not even once. They just dealt with it however they were dealing with it and didn't let on to it bothering them. Hell, she wasn't even sure it *did* bother them, this whole *sharing a temporary lover* thing, and that made it all the more complicated because it made her all the more comfortable with sticking around a little longer.

Which just wasn't an option. Even if she had seen Joe Delany earlier that day, when she'd hiked a few miles up the hill to search for a water source and found him directing a trail maintenance team. He'd asked her about the job. Again. He'd asked the first time a few days after they had met and after one more visit to the house and two phone calls each to Dec and Micah about her, Lily had no doubt in her mind that the Environmental Education Coordinator position for the Black Reef Mountains Park Rangers was available to her.

Another complicated element to the whole matter of her needing to go home in a week. But Mia had promised that the business was doing just fine without her, and when she'd emailed over a couple of invoices for Lily to sign, Lily had noticed that Mia was doing better than she'd been able to do in the last two months. Fine, one week and no thinking of home.

"Forget brownies. I want to eat you up," Dec said, coming from behind her as she tried to swipe a brownie from his plate on the counter. "And no testing — those are for later." She very overtly bit into one of the brownies and gave him a no doubt chocolatey smile.

"Better to ask for forgiveness... How are you so good at this stuff, anyway? I mean, I can follow a recipe, but you're good."

The smile on Dec's face was sad. "Necessity," he said, "like most things. When Dad worked eighty hours a week to put food on the table, you put food on the table. I started because I had to and, when I could afford good food and ingredients, well, I realized I enjoyed it."

Lily sighed and placed the brownie down before hugging him to her. It was a funny thought that she, all of a hundred and forty pounds soaking wet, might protect the big, hulking survival man with his search dogs and military training, but Dec accepted the hug and wrapped his arms around her in return before kissing her on the head.

Finally, Lily pulled back, just in time to watch Dec take a bite out of her brownie. She glared but he just laughed.

"Better to ask for forgiveness," he said. "Come on, Micah's got the horses saddled up. Let's go." He slid the brownies into a food container and they headed out to the barn, where three horses stood ready for them. Micah and Dec had their favorites, of course. In Micah's case, that was Aranck, which translated to stars, like the thousands of white spots that decorated Aranck's black coat. Dec had gone a little more literal with Cisco and the horse she'd been using these past few days was a chestnut mare named Cee Cee.

The routine had become quite familiar and Lily hopped into the saddle, following the two men down the mountain and toward the Hut. They passed two of her research sites, a ropes course and three small lakes, which shimmered in the late afternoon sun, catching the glimpses of gold and red from the trees. They took a few unfamiliar turns then they were there, standing before what could only be the Hut.

"What the ever-loving hell is that?" Lily couldn't keep back her disbelief. Not only was it not a hut, it wasn't much of anything. The cabin, or house, or building was caving in at the top and there was no glass in any of the windows. A porch, or rather, what had once been a porch, sagged, with three of the five steps cracked through. A whimpering sound gave her the distinct impression that some sort of animal was inside.

"That's the Hut," Micah said on a laugh. He dismounted and helped her down from her horse, taking the two sets of reins and Dec's when he hit the ground. "The whole point of the thing is for it to be dangerous."

"Why?" She took a hesitant step closer. The damn thing really looked like it was an inch away from total collapse and she didn't have any desire to be in the area when that happened.

"Danger assessment training," Dec explained. "If you come upon a place that you could use for shelter, the last thing you want is to put your foot through the floor and end up with a broken ankle. We send in small teams to try to make the place safe to sleep for the night, reinforce the frame, get the animals out. That sort of thing."

She raised an eyebrow. "That seems….dangerous."

Dec grinned. "It totally is. But that's why people take this course — they want to know how to handle any situation, and the most important step, in survival, in first aid, in any of it, is securing your safety first. You can't help anyone else if you're dead kind of thing."

It made sense, even if she had every intention of staying far the fuck away from this creepy old place.

"So, why are you going to tear it down then?" she asked.

Micah shrugged. "We've had some pretty rough storms this year, especially one big snowfall back in April that knocked the shit out the place. We're worried it'll be the kind of dangerous we can't contain." He took her hand and smiled down at her, that warm, rich smile that made her stomach heat and her body unconsciously lean closer to his. "But there's something way better to show you. Come on."

He led her and Dec followed as they skirted the edge of the — Christ on a cauliflower, she couldn't even think of it as a house — and walked around to a small grove of pines. They pushed through the clearing and came upon...

The most beautiful vista she had ever seen. The ground leveled off into a small field and overlooked the sight of the Black Reef Mountains rising up over one of the lakes. The scene was breath taking, gorgeous, more real than a postcard, and yet she half-wanted to reach out and see if she was touching a photograph, because truly, had there ever been anything more beautiful in the world than this view?

"It's incredible," she said, her voice just above a whisper. She took both of their hands and squeezed them tightly before moving to sit on the patch of grass that overlooked the vista. Dirt and rocks dotted the far side of the hill, which rolled to the cliff's edge some hundred feet away. But they were safe here and she'd never felt safer in her life than when she sat between the two of them, eyes on the far view, fingers tangled in both Micah's and Dec's.

Micah stroked her hand gently and Dec wrapped his arm around her waist and all of a sudden she wasn't thinking just about the vista, but also about how close each of them were to her, how much she wanted something she wasn't sure if she was allowed to want. She'd slept with both of them several times since the first night, but always alone, always separately, as if they were all pretending to be okay with the stirring, very temporary, madness between them. But now that she was here, in the wild open nature, in the wild open air, Lily wasn't sure she could resist anymore. She wanted them both. *Together.*

"You're thinking so hard I'm half-expecting the ground to crack," Micah said on a laugh. "What's going on in that pretty little head?"

Lily didn't answer. How could she answer when it was clear that they weren't touching the whole 'sleeping with her together' topic again and she wasn't going to be the one to bring it up, no matter how much she wanted it? And given that her nipples were growing hard and her breasts swollen and her breath shallow, she couldn't deny that she wanted it.

"Lily." Dec brought his hand low to her back and that just made the heat in her body swirl to new heights all over again. She was like a volcano around these men, both of them so capable of making her come again and again, and when she was with them at the same time... "You're going to have to be honest with us or this is never going to work." When he said it like that, she could almost believe, almost pretend that he meant beyond the scope of the week before them, that he meant they needed to find some way to *make this work* in the long term, in the forever.

Forever. Whoa. She wasn't here for forever, not by any stretch of the imagination. How could she do forever when she hadn't thought past the next order of peonies or the next rent bill in so many years? And, yet, now that the idea had taken some sort of form in her head, it was a little sticky and more than a little dangerous. Because she'd thought she would have forever before and she'd only gotten six years of grief and pain and sadness and she wasn't going to go through that, not again.

Though, of course, everything that had happened with Daniel had been a million miles away from this, well, whatever this was, and she was in no position to compare them, but the end result would be the same. She would still wake up alone and sooner than later.

But, for now, she could pretend that Dec was talking about making it work in a way that didn't have such an encroaching deadline and so she took both of their hands and gave them long, lingering strokes.

"You're right," Lily began, trying to keep the nerves from showing in her voice. "Maddy said this was all about communication and I guess she knows what she's talking about, so here goes... I know we're trying to keep this as uncomplicated as possible, of course. But...I want you both again. Together. Like the first night." It seemed once the words had started rolling out of her mouth they weren't stopping and she couldn't keep from blurting what was on her mind.

"I want to feel full and stretched and I want you guys to be rough. I know this makes things a little more complicated, but—"

"Lily, if that's what you want. We want to make you happy," Micah cut in. He glanced over at Dec as if looking for reassurance and Dec nodded.

"Whatever that takes, we'll try it," he said. "Does that make you feel a little better?"

Lily released a shaky breath, tension easing from her shoulders. "That was easier than I expected," she admitted on a laugh. "So are we done talking now or—"

Dec's hand was on her ass and squeezing hard before she even got the words out. He hauled her onto his lap, his already hard erection poking against her, making her desire mount and her need to be filled hard and fast and over and over again rise, especially when Micah took her face in his large, rough hands and brought her in for a bruising, blistering kiss.

They were so much, everything about their touch set her body to flame in unique and impossible ways. Micah made her burn low and white hot, while Dec seared a wild fire through her body. Together, they were a natural disaster.

It was chilly on the mountaintop, with the wind from the valley below casting gales in their direction, but Lily barely felt the bite of the air, not with the heat building between her legs, making her part her lips to Micah's tongue, making her breasts feel heavy and swollen as Dec palmed them in his hand. Then he was pulling at the buttons on her flannel shirt to the T-shirt below, slipping one hand under the hem and running his fingers up her skin.

She bucked at the contact, jerking even harder when Micah's mouth came down to her neck and she sucked in a breath at the zing of pleasure shooting across her body. At her motion, Dec's cock gave a throb and she pressed back against him, loving the way he felt, loving how she knew she could get a reaction out of both of these men, powerful, strong, losing control to her touch.

"More…" Her voice. Christ on a… Fuck, was that her voice? Lily was certain her moans could be heard a county away and she didn't give a good goddamn, not when Dec took over kissing her neck and Micah slid her shirt up to press achingly slow, teasing kisses to her skin, to her belly, to the low mounds of her breasts. Her breathing was short and her body was slipping to a horizontal position on the ground, which neither man seemed to have a problem with.

Because Dec was kissing her now, bruising, blustering kisses, and Micah had moved down the length of her body to kiss the inside of her denim-clad thighs. It wasn't enough. It wasn't anywhere close to enough. She felt poised on the edge and ready to burst with fire and need, if they would only let her, only take her the way she so desperately wanted to be taken.

But it was clear that neither of the two men had all that much control right at the moment, because Dec's movements were blazing and his kisses demanding and Micah was running down the length of her legs as though he couldn't wait to bury himself inside her and, damn it, that was all Lily wanted.

"Fucking teases," she moaned, her voice breathy and low. Dec chuckled by her ear, a potent, masculine sound, but Micah was too busy unbuttoning her jeans and yanking them down to answer. He pulled them halfway down her legs, muttering to himself about how *fucking tight women's pants were*, then he was toying with her scrap of panties, the pair she hadn't even thought she would wear while out in Montana working in the dirt. They were dark red, trimmed with gold and a little golden bow at the top and soft, smooth silk. Which, of course, meant they were perfect for getting fucked on a mountainside by two warriors.

"So fucking sexy," Micah murmured. "I'll never get tired of looking at you all spread out like this." And without another word, not a promise or a warning of any kind, he buried himself between her legs. He sucked hard at the silk panties, the scrap of fabric brushing against her swollen clit in an erotic, sensual caress, one bursting in contrast to the roughness with which Micah lapped at the wet fabric covering her pussy, as if he were starved and she were a feast just waiting for him.

"Lift up." He didn't wait for her but lifted her hips off the ground and yanked her panties down her thighs, pulling the silk and her jeans as far down as he could. They bunched around her ankles, fucking skinny jeans, but then Micah was back on her cunt and she couldn't think about her own name, let alone the fashion industry.

But she wanted both of them, here, totally with her, so she pulled Dec down for a rough kiss then slid her hand across the zipper on his jeans. He was hard and throbbing and she couldn't help but tease, tracing the outline of his cock through his boxer briefs, stroking him and watching in fascination as he responded to her touch.

"Off." The word made Dec grin and he somehow managed to make scrambling out of his jeans look smug, but then he had them down and she had a prime view of his hardness, bobbing just out of reach of her mouth. She tried to move for it, but Dec shifted just a little too far away.

"What do you say?" he asked, as if he wasn't hard as a rock and just inches from her mouth. Son of a bitch still had way too much self-control for her liking. But Lily couldn't deny that she liked this game they were playing, and so said exactly what she knew he wanted to hear. What she wanted to say.

"Please may I suck your cock?"

Dec brushed the seeping head over her bottom lip and a pulse of electricity burned her entire spine, pleasure lighting to fire within her at the simple motion. She glanced up at him from what she knew to be hooded eyes, half from the way Micah was devouring her, sending shockwaves of need through her body and half from how she knew she was making Dec feel. He groaned audibly and stroked his cock across her lip again.

"I can't think when you look at me like that, Lils," he said. "Like you'll do anything I ask you to with a goddamn smile on your face."

At that, she did smile. "Maybe I will," she said. "Why don't you come and find out?"

"More like find out and come," Dec murmured, but the humor was all gone, his face that of a man trying desperately to leash control.

"Oh, God, Micah." Lily lost her concentration on Dec's throbbing cock when Micah slid a finger deep inside her, joined by another, then a third in quick succession. "Please…oh, God…please?" She didn't even know what the hell she was begging for, only that if she didn't get it soon she might just damn well go insane.

But Micah seemed to know and slid his free hand up under her hips, somehow managing to turn her body so she was on her hands and knees, without ever losing contact between his fingers and her pulsing pussy. He leaned over her back, pressing deep inside her as his weight came over her shoulder, a reminder of how purely masculine, muscled and powerful he was.

"I want you to come in my mouth," he said, "then you'll get fucked. But only if you do as I ask you to."

She nodded, unable to form words as his mouth now attacked her from behind, his fingers still sliding in and out of her body without mercy or pause. Barely able to think, she managed to get her head up enough to call Dec over to her. Finally, finally, he came close enough so that she could take his cock into her mouth and suck him, wrapping her tongue around the velvety feel of his hardness, making her moan and squirm and ache with the feeling of Micah's fingers and Dec's hardness inside her all at the same time.

Then she was spiraling, losing control to the insane onslaught of sensation. She pulled free of Dec's cock and bowed forward, fisting the ground as she came in wave after wave of pleasure, spilling hot release all over Micah's mouth and fingers. He slid free of her body, running a wet finger across her ass before he kissed her there.

"Good girl," he groaned. Then, from behind her, came the telltale sound of his zipper and the ripping of a condom wrapper. He positioned himself at her wet, still throbbing hole and continued the slow caress of his fingers across her ass. "What do you think, Lily, do you want to be filled in both holes and suck Dec's cock all at the same time?" His finger, still slick with her juices, edged the rim of her ass and Lily couldn't keep the sigh from escaping her mouth. "I'll take that as a yes."

He slid his finger in first, slow, so gentle that it make her ache, made the pleasure start in her toes and wind up her spine in tendrils of kindling flame. Then he had his finger entirely lodged in her ass, his cock right there, right at the entrance to her pussy. He slipped inside her at the same moment that Dec pressed into her mouth.

She came in an instant. The insane sensations of all three holes filled and stretching her tight pushed her right over the edge and she screamed around Dec's cock, shuddering and coming hard. But they weren't done with her and Micah began a slow assault on her pussy with his cock, still stroking his finger in and out of her tight hole, as Dec slid hard and deep into her mouth, his movements rough and demanding and achingly erotic.

Another orgasm was already building, the pressure and heat rising up her body, making her bow and moan around Dec's cock. She arched her back, so desperate for more, more contact, more pressure, more *something*. Dec popped free of her mouth and slid his cock along her cheek, slick with her spit and his pre-cum. She glanced up at him and he pulled back for a moment. Then slapped his cock across her cheek.

The ground came out from under her at the demanding, fucking hot movement and she screamed, not muffled by his cock this time as she pulsed, coming hard around Micah's cock. Dec didn't give her the chance to say anything, because he slid back inside her then they were both fucking her hard and with abandon, no more steady rhythm, no more gentle caressing, rough and demanding and promising.

"One more time, baby," Micah demanded. "Come with us, come around my cock while I'm filling you deep."

She shook her head. Her body was spent and she could barely keep up with their driving pace, but there it was there, anyway, the beginning of an intense, overwhelming orgasm and Lily tried to just hold on tight for the ride.

"Yes, you can." Dec had the voice of a soldier now. "And you will, Lily. Be a good girl for us and come again." His voice broke and she could feel him give over to the pleasure. Then he was thrusting once, twice, once more. "Fuck, Lily, I'm coming…" She kept him in her mouth and sucked as he pumped thick strands across her tongue and down her throat. Micah was losing his control, too, and she turned to look at him at the exact moment she felt him slide another slick finger against the entrance to her ass and…

"*Fuck.*"

She burst, combusting in a volcanic eruption of pleasure that made fireworks explode behind her eyes, blasting, blowing, sending her careering right off the edge and into the delicious white-hot abyss. Distantly, she registered Micah's final thrust and the condom filled hot inside her as he gave over to the pleasure, pumping one more time before his movements slowed and he slumped over, keeping his weight off her back.

With a gentleness she didn't know he possessed, he pulled his fingers, then his cock free from her body. Her eyes were closed, but a moment later she felt a moist tissue against her skin then soft, gentle lips, so distinct, against her belly and thighs.

After a long moment, all cleaned up and able to get her breath back into her lungs, Lily slowly opened her eyes and looked up at the two men beside her. Dec was sitting up and Micah was lying back on his elbows, just looking out at the sunset across the valley. She couldn't even bring herself to care about how much time they'd spent out here, not with the incredible pleasure they'd just given her. How on earth was she going to say goodbye to this?

"Well," she said, instead of going down that path of self-pity and guilt, "I think the view is now officially my second-favorite thing about this mountain."

Chapter Twelve

Not only were they late to Triple Diamond, but it was completely obvious why. Lily had already given hugs and accepted a drink before popping into the bathroom, where she discovered that about half the fallen leaves in the entire Black Reef Mountain range had made it into her hair and that the buttons on her flannel jacket were all off by one. But that wasn't what made it so obvious. No, even a perfunctory glance in the mirror was enough to highlight her…well, her *glow*. Her face shone, her smile was genuine and she just looked…well, like she'd been making love to the two sexiest men she'd ever met on a freaking mountainside.

Fucking them. She'd been fucking them. *Not* making love, because she was leaving in a week and she refused to leave her heart here when she went back to San Francisco. Plus, the complication of falling for two men at the same time was an added bonus round of *not going to deal with that*. Instead, she tried, in vain, to fix the long fishtail braid that had definitely not survived their tryst, re-buttoned her shirt and walked out of the bathroom.

And straight into Maddy, who had clearly been waiting for her on the other side of the door, if the smug and none-too-subtle expression on her face was anything to go by. Her sister had always been ruthless. It had gotten her ahead in school and her career and led to a pretty badass second career of running the Triple Diamond Events Company. But, right now, Maddy had turned all that ruthlessness on her, and Lily knew she was headed for an interrogation of epic proportions.

"We're going on a walk," Maddy said. "And you are going to spill everything, Miss." They walked through the kitchen and Maddy stopped to grab two more beers from the fridge before they headed into the cool night. The sky had grown into sharp darkness in the time it took them to get down from the hill from where the Hut was located and it smelled like heavy rain was in the air with thick clouds covering the night sky. Still, there was no beating the delicious smell of fall in the mountains, now coupled with hay and the clean, natural scent of animals. Lucy—Lucifer, a little gray cat—wove between Maddy's legs and followed them to the pond at the far end of the patio, where Maddy dropped into a chair. She motioned for Lily to sit down and she did with marked slowness, anticipating the coming interview.

"Where are Micah and Dec?" she asked, all of a sudden aware of the quietness around them, as if there weren't four grown men wandering around somewhere, causing trouble, no doubt.

"We've got a coyote problem," Maddy said, pursing her lips. "They don't live far outside the ranch grounds, but they've been getting bolder, even though the season's winding down, and the Christian and Ryder are worried about the livestock. They mentioned asking Dec and Micah about tracking it."

Of course they did. Because Dec and Micah were the best survival experts and tracking this side of the Mississippi — did that apply here? It didn't matter. Either way, her guys would know what to do. And she only used the term *her guys* to differentiate between Maddy's guys. *Right. Obviously. Not a head trip at all.*

When that train of thought departed, she was just left with the low, uncomfortable worry of knowing they were tracking a predator in the middle of the woods in the dark. Of course, that was no less than half of their camp training program, but the knowledge of that didn't ease her worry much.

"Okay, we're done with the chit-chat," Maddy said. "I heard that Joe Delany has taken to asking you about the new Environmental Educator Program coordinator position and you haven't flat out told him no. So, either you start with that, or the fact that you clearly got fucked six ways to Sunday before you got here. Which one first?"

Lily sighed. Maddy was good. Lily had kept from mentioning the job and Joe Delany's persistence on purpose, but this wasn't San Francisco. It was Wolf Creek, Montana, and word got around fast. Still, from the look in Maddy's eyes right then, Lily couldn't be sure if talking about the job was the safer topic. Rock and a hard place — where she'd literally been no more than an hour ago.

"I'm sleeping with both of them." She blurted it, because it wasn't going to come out any other way.

"So I gathered." Maddy's voice was without judgment — obviously, since the woman was the poster girl for three-ring-circus relationships, but a hint of concern did manage to sneak through.

"That obvious?" she asked, pursing her lips. Of course she was that obvious. She'd been working ten-hour research days in the woods by herself and spending the rest of her time with Dec or Micah or both. They hadn't needed to hide what was between them because there was no one to hide it from. *Not* that she could have hidden anything from Maddy, because that was a no-go, for sure.

Maddy raised an eyebrow, an amused smile curling on her lips. "Hello, pot, I'm kettle." She stuck out her hand and Lily just laughed.

"You haven't walked in on us yet, so we're still not even." The laugh turned into a sigh. "I'm leaving in a week, Mads," she said, her voice quiet. "Logically, rationally, I know this. Right? My research will be completed in a week and then I head home to finalize lab reports. But…"

"You don't want to go home." Madison said this in the matter-of-fact tone of voice that could only come from someone with first-hand experience. "Wolf Creek does that, Lils. Triple Diamond does that. This whole place is a siren's call. Next thing you know, we're changing up our entire lives just to find a way to stick around."

"What if they don't want me to stick around?" It was barely a whisper and the sound surprised her almost more than it surprised Maddy. Because, deep down, wasn't that why she'd been dodging Joe Delany's calls? Sure, she had the shop back in San Francisco, but was that going to be enough to drag her home after everything this silly little mountain range had become to her in the past weeks? No, the undercurrent of her fear and hesitation was right there, the whisper hanging like smoke on the air before them, like the heavy storm clouds gathering high above their heads.

"They'd be fools not to want you to stay here," Maddy said, her voice almost as quiet as Lily's had been. "And I really don't think either of them is a fool. It may take them longer — this whole thing, it's new to Dec and Micah in a way it wasn't new to Ryder and Christian. Things might have to get a little tangled before they're cleared up."

She paused and put her beer down, taking both of Lily's hands in her own. "Either way, it's not about what they want, it's about what you want. Do you want to go after that job, Lily? Because if you do, I'm right there with you. You can stay here. We have guest houses and I'll make Ryder and Christian learn some discretion." The light blush rising up her neck indicated that maybe it was Maddy who needed to learn some discretion, but she barreled on. "No matter what they say or do, if you want that job, you'll be welcome here for as long as you need, Lily. For forever. Nothing would make me happier than for you to come live with me here, if that made you happy, too."

Tears hedged the corners of Lily's eyes and she blinked them back. Maddy had been home a few times to pack up her life, but being here by her side and hearing her sister's adamant declaration of love and unconditional support made her heart swell and she pulled Maddy into a hug. They held tight to each other for several moments and when she finally pulled back, neither of them had dry eyes.

"I think I'm going to call Joe in the morning," Lily said, and those simple words lifted a weight from her shoulders she hadn't even realized was there. "Just to talk," she added quickly, when Maddy's face lit up. Maddy's smile remained, though, becoming something a little more real and more powerful.

"And the guys?" she asked, gentle, calm.

"I'll talk to them," Lily replied. Because what else could she do? Whether they wanted her to stay or not, if she did like what Joe Delany said, if she could somehow start the track to maybe even staying in this crazy place for a while, well, she was going to need to figure out a way to make things between all three of them clear. They could very well ask her to leave their lives forever, but they were sharing the same plot of land as the Triple Diamond Ranch and would never be that far apart.

The idea of being *any* apart made her heart feel squirmy and slippery and she squeezed Maddy's hand in reassurance.

Or maybe Maddy squeezed hers. "Whatever you need," she said. "I'll always be there. Just give me the call."

Lily didn't doubt it for a second.

* * * *

They had been following Christian Harlow and Ryder Dean in complete silence for nearly fifteen minutes when Dec realized why that was so strange to him. He'd spent most of his life around men. Growing up, it had been him and dad and two brothers. He'd gone into the military, then into search and rescue, before opening a business that in large part catered to men, with his best friend, a man. His longest relationship with a woman had been long-distance and even Maddy Hollis, whom he cared for deeply, remained a bit of an enigma to him.

Which was why it had taken him a quarter of an hour to understand why this Silence Among Men thing was so weird.

Lily. Lily Hollis, who'd been in his life long enough to throw everything upside and backward. Lily, who could read botany books for hours in comfortable quiet, but refused to allow anything resembling the macho-man, vaguely uncomfortable silence just like the kind Dec was all too aware of now. Lily always made sounds, a snicker or smug laugh low beneath her breath. A gasp at the information she was reading. The swish of her long, dark hair from one side of her head to the other in a waterfall of movement.

The thing Dec wasn't entirely sure of was whether or not Lily made more sounds than other women, or if he was just more aware of them when it came to her. He was certainly aware of how she smelled when she walked into a room, like lavender and pine and fresh dirt, the way her arms felt, wrapping around his neck when he sat at the computer desk, filling out Survival Camp registration information. Details of who she was and how she acted had been filing away in his brain for days, weeks — long enough to fill up his mind and make him crazed with thoughts of her.

"I'm thinking they're getting through the fence right around here," Ryder said, breaking Dec's concentration and throwing him right back into the deep end of why having feelings for Lily was such a bad idea. Not that he did. Because he didn't have feelings for her. This was all just sex and friendship, no love.

Ha, he couldn't even lie the words to himself properly, because it was so freaking obvious by the way she made him melt, just a little, when she walked into a room. He thought of her more than he thought of Aubrey and, given that Aubrey had pretty much haunted him since the day he'd driven all the way back from North Dakota, Dec had to take that to mean *something*.

Fine, whether he was admitting to having the feelings or not, *if* he did want something more from her than whatever they had now, Christian and Ryder were reason enough to back the fuck off. Because they did just about anything Maddy asked of them. If Maddy didn't think Dec and Micah were good enough for her sister, then they were gone, simple as.

They? Right, that was another added complicated to the already way too much what the fuckery that was going on. So, Dec turned to where Ryder was standing, scanning the ground with a small handheld machine... *Why am I doing that? Oh, yeah.* Dec really needed to focus his attention back to the matter at hand. Not that either Ryder or Christian could pretend they didn't know what had happened the minute before their trio had arrived at the ranch, because, God, it had been so fucking obvious. But if they weren't going to acknowledge it then he sure as shit wasn't about to broach the subject.

"You call the fence company out?" Micah asked. "They could probably give you some better info on keeping the right wildlife out."

Ah, yes, they had been talking about the Triple Diamond coyote problem, hadn't they? That was, without a doubt, a safer topic of conversation than the way Lily felt wrapping her mouth around his cock and sucking hard.

"They said they'd send a guy from Helena," Christian replied, a scowl on his face. "Which means at least a week till we get an appointment, so we just thought we'd check with you guys, unless you're not as good at this whole tracking thing" — he held up his fingers in air quotes — "as you want everyone to think you are."

Dec just laughed. "Green isn't your color, Harlow," he said, "but we could probably squeeze you into one of our beginner classes, if you're not scared."

Christian flipped him off, using his other hand to push his hair out of his face. It wasn't nearly as long as Micah's, whose current ponytail reached halfway down his back, but long hair or not, no one was going to fuck with either man. Damn, that was some pretty terrible word choice if he'd heard any, since it sent his mind spiraling right back to the way Lily felt, wrapped around him, to the expression she made when she came, hard and shuddering around his cock, to...

"I know it's not coyote piss that's putting that expression on your face." Ryder clapped him on the back and shrugged his shoulders. "Not much we can do here until the fence guys come, right?"

"Pretty much," Micah said. Before he could add any more though, Ryder squeezed Dec's shoulder tight and got all big and puffy, like the human race hadn't sustained thousands of years of evolution since the blowfish.

"You didn't bring us out here to look at the fence." The statement was simple, but, come on, Dec could pretty much feel the guys' radiating heat and he just sighed. They'd both known this was coming. After all, Ryder and Christian were ass over boots in love with Lily's sister and they'd do anything they could to make Maddy, and by extension her family, happy.

"Obviously not," Christian said on a low, guttural laugh. "So do you want to go first or should we get right down to it?"

"We're sleeping with Maddy's sister." Dec got to the point, though when he phrased it like that, it felt crude and rough and...somehow wrong, against his lips. Because it wasn't just that and it hadn't been just that since the day she had walked through the door and upended at the very least his life but probably Micah's too.

"And what are you going to do about it?" Ryder put in. It was kind of fun, watching Ryder Dean and Christian Harlow play the overprotective — brother? — role. They'd been the kids everyone's parents had warned them away from back in high school. Troublemakers and Casanovas. Though, of course, Dec knew a thing or two about being labeled at first glance.

"She's leaving in a week," Micah replied, folding his arms and making himself big. He was big, bigger than the three of them and they all cleared the six-foot mark. Yeah, Dec was happy to have Micah on his side in a fight. "There's nothing for us to do about it. She's not going to magically decide to stay on the ranch her mysterious uncle left her in his will." Which was exactly how things had gone down with Madison Hollis and why Christian and Ryder had this overprotective air around them they'd never had before.

"What if she does?" Ryder challenged. "What if she's here more often than you think? You guys have been busting our balls for years over sharing lovers, but this is new ground and I just want you both to know the rules. Will you both keep dating her, or are you going to make her pick?"

The words were a punch in the gut and Dec winced. Obviously it was in the hypothetical, since Lily had been adamant since the get-go about needing to return to her shop and her home. But what if she did visit a lot? After all, her sister lived here now and there was something to be said for escaping city life. Confusion swamped his already stretched emotions and he looked at Micah, who suddenly didn't appear as big or as solid as he had a moment ago. There was no doubt about it, Lily Hollis had definitely thrown a sexy-as-sin wrench into the works of their lives.

"You guys need to figure that out," Christian said, his voice firm. "We're telling you because we know and you know it 'cause you're the ones who broke up the fight where we nearly beat the shit out of each other for both wanting Maddy to ourselves. Well, it doesn't always work that way. In the end, you have to remember who you're doing it all for."

Then, to Dec's surprise, he stuck out his hand. "You're good men," he said. "Both of you. And we're obviously not going to pass judgment on the type of relationship you decide. But you do have to be open and communicative or someone will get hurt. And if Lily gets hurt, well, you know we have to kick your ass."

"You can try," Dec said, but he accepted first Christian's then Ryder's handshake. Micah did the same then the other two men took off down the hill, giving them a little bit of privacy under the cool, cloudy skies. Rain was in the air and electricity crackled in the far-off mountains.

"Shit." Micah's voice sounded like the thunder coming their direction and Dec sighed, nodding his head.

"What are we doing here, Micah?" he asked. "I mean, yeah, she's taking off, but she'll be back and…it's just a big old clusterfuck right now. Obviously, they're right, I don't want anything to happen to her, but we can't keep this up."

Micah just sighed and looked up at the clouds. "You want to make her choose," he said, his tone without judgment. "That won't be an easy conversation to have, Dec. It's going to suck, no matter what happens. I don't know how we can expect that to work."

"I don't know how we can expect *this* to work," Dec replied in exasperation, not at Micah so much as the crazy confusion of things going on around them. "I mean, how can they do it, really?" He jerked his chin in the direction Ryder and Christian had gone. "How can they share the love of their lives with each other and not struggle every single day, wondering and doubting?"

"Is Lily the love of your life?" Micah asked, his tone softening just a little. This question was no punch in the gut but a flame that started at his toes and burned him up, consuming and demanding reprieve. Because, of course, hadn't he been asking himself something similar since the moment he'd lain eyes on her?

"Not yet," he admitted. It was the truth. "But I'm terrified that she could be." Terrified because this was all mired in their shared relationship with one woman, terrified because he had survived the leaving of first his mother then Aubrey and if Lily walked out of his life it would rip him apart worse than either of those two absences ever had. "What about you?"

Micah, who had long ago believed he wasn't deserving of *love*, rolled his head on his shoulders, looking like a mountain stretching its neck.

"It's real for me," he said, stark, honest, raw. "Whatever that means, however you want to phrase it, it's real for me."

"So we lay it on the table," Dec replied, trying not to let Micah's words hit him where it hurt. "And we see what she has to say. If and when she comes back here, it'll have to be different. We can't do this for our whole lives, Micah."

"No matter what, it has to be up to her," Micah replied. "And I can't lose you, too, Dec. Whatever she says, yes or no, up or down, you or me, I can't lose you as my best friend."

Dec had to grit his teeth to keep from letting the emotion at the back of his throat overwhelm him and break free. He clapped Micah on the back and just nodded his agreement, even as fear and pain and guilt settled low in his belly. Because if this went wrong — and it had all the potential to go really, really, wrong — he could end up losing the two most important people in his life.

Chapter Thirteen

Something was up. Micah's silence wasn't anything new, though most of the time his quiet was a comfortable, peaceful kind, and right now Lily could practically see the lightning crackling around his body, signs of his unease and discomfort. Even the normally loquacious Dec was riding beside her back up the mountain with very little to say and the whole thing was so odd that Lily opened and shut her mouth several times, unsure of how to break the unusual tension.

After a very long quiet, she settled on a humorous topic. "So did the guys threaten to kick your ass or something?" She and Maddy had headed into the kitchen to get dinner together and the four men had stayed out in the fields for far longer than she would have thought it necessary to track a few coyotes, especially for the supposed best trackers in the mountains.

Dec scoffed. "They tried to. Don't tell them I said this, but it turned into more of a heart-to-heart."

Lily just laughed, imaging the four bulky, hulking men standing around talking about their feelings. Of course, that was adhering to all sorts of stereotypes about men and manliness and she knew for a damn fact that Dec and Micah both had feelings to spare, but the visual was striking.

"Well, Maddy and I had a good chat," she said, feeling much more at ease than she had a moment before. There was nothing going on here except a little good old-fashioned quiet. She was definitely reading into it being something more.

"Ooh, safeguard your ego, Micah," Dec said, looking over at Micah, whose stoic face cut into a small grin. She revised her earlier statement. *Something's definitely up.* The question was what?

"Nothing like that." She edged Cee Cee closer and swatted him on the arm. "I was going to wait to tell you guys until we got back, but I'm thinking of talking to Joe Delany tomorrow. Nothing serious, of course, just to find out what sort of requirements the job entails. I know Mia would love to run the shop on her own for as long as I'd let her, so I'm not worried about racing home, if he'd let me test things out for a few weeks. Mads says I can stay in one of the guest houses on the ranch then figure out if I want to make things permanent."

Micah stopped short first and Aranck whinnied his disapproval at the sudden movement. Cisco, unbothered, casually pulled off to the side and Lily somehow found herself staring down two large horses and two seemingly larger men.

"What the hell is going on right now?" She didn't mean to snap, but there was so much, between the way they'd both given her all that pleasure up on the hillside, to the overwhelming conversation she'd had with her sister about maybe uprooting her entire life, to the weird simmering tension between them, that Lily just didn't have a whole lot left. "Because clearly something is going on and if it's going to make you both weird and moody all night then I damn well want to know what it is."

Another beat of silence. In the far-distant mountains, thunder rolled.

Micah spoke first, his words more sigh than speech. "Christian and Ryder got real with us, Lily. They wanted to know what we see happening here, in the future and all that. They just meant when you come back to visit Maddy, but now you're thinking of staying here, so it looks like we have to answer this question sooner than we thought."

And though she already had a *very* good idea as to where this conversation was going, Lily gritted her teeth and asked, "And what question might that be?"

Dec replied before Micah got the chance, "This thing between us, Lils, it's…complicated. Maybe some men are cut out for a life like this, but I just don't think I am." He looked over at Micah, who slowly, but very definitively, shook his head. "We just wanted to lay it all out on the table, ya know? We can't play this game where you date us both for the next however long you decide to live here, or whenever you visit."

His voice dropped low and she could see all those shattered glimpses of the man who had been left by the women who loved him too many times.

"It's a self-preservation thing," he said. "It can't be both."

Such an innocuous statement. *It can't be both.* Like she couldn't have a cookie and a cupcake. *It can't be both,* like a client couldn't get winter and summer flowers in the same bouquet. *It can't be both,* like she couldn't keep the two men she loved in her life for any longer than two weeks.

Loved.

Holy shit.

The panic turned to anger in a second and she gripped Cee Cee's reins tight in her hands.

"You want me to choose?" Her voice was scary calm and in the ghostly light from the thick clouds above, Lily could see they were both startled by her tone. "Oh, no, you don't get to make me choose. No fucking way. Here's the deal, gentlemen." She overemphasized the word and Dec winced. "You're allowed to break up with me. Both of you, either of you. You're allowed to say, 'Hey, Lils, it's just not working out. It's not you, it's me. I'm afraid of commitment.' Whatever the fuck. But you do not get to stand there—" Oh, her voice was definitely rising now. "Stand there and tell me that I have to pick one of you, like you haven't both guided me into a new life, like you haven't both helped me see the light at the end of the tunnel after all that I've lost. Like you haven't both made me fall face fucking first in love with you these past days." Her voice cracked and the waterworks started, silent tears streaming down her face. Or maybe that was the light splatter of drizzle on her face. So fucking fitting.

"You love us?" Micah asked, his voice so soft she could barely hear it. "Both of us?"

But Lily was done talking now. Her heart ached and burned and froze all at the same time and she turned Cee Cee away from the two men and back toward Triple Diamond.

"I'm going to stay with Madison tonight," she said. "Maybe I'll be back in the morning."

"Lily, it's about to storm. It's not safe," Dec said, his voice almost pleading, fear coloring the edges. Right at that moment, she didn't give a damn. Because it hadn't really resonated until right now, until she stared down the barrel of the gun, just what it meant to love both of them, just what it meant to have that love questioned, as if she could just snap her fingers and stop loving two men with equal parts passion and respect and joy and lust and everything else all rolled into one. And the fact that it had been these men themselves asking the fucking impossible question made the pain cut so deep in her chest that she wondered if she was even still breathing.

"I swear to God, if either one of you follow me, I'll be on the first plane out of here in the morning," she said, and without another word she was down the hill, pushing Cee Cee toward Maddy and away from the two men who so very carelessly held her heart.

* * * *

Micah didn't worry about much. He knew how to live in the wilderness for years, if he had to, could fashion food and shelter out of anything that could be found in the woods and could disappear off the grid overnight, should reason arise. He had long ago come to the conclusion that borrowing trouble only ever made things worse and his instinct as to when a problem was real or just looked real had very rarely steered him wrong.

So, the fact that he was worried at all, panic and fear gnawing at his stomach like midnight monsters under the bed, made him worried all over again.

They hadn't heard from Lily in hours. He had wanted to follow her, wanted to damn her threats to leave to hell and follow her right down to the Triple Diamond Ranch, demand she…demand she *what*? The hurt in her eyes when they'd told her she had to pick one of them was as raw and gutting as a fish knife to the flesh and one glance at Dec had said everything. They needed to give her the chance to work things out or she would never forgive them. Besides, Maddy Hollis had been through everything before and if anyone in the world could offer some sage advice on unorthodox relationships, it would be her.

Except Lily hadn't sent either one of them so much as a text or a basic call, and though he ached with the hurt he had seen in her eyes, the hurt he and Dec had caused her, Micah was more worried than anything else. He and Dec had come home, begrudgingly, and not ten minutes later, the storm that had been threatening all night had finally opened up and the skies had crashed down, wild and maddening around them. Trees whipped in the gales of winds and water hit the windows with the force of bullets upon the glass. He'd gone so far as to grab the puppies and other dogs from the barn, just as Lily had done the week before, and pulled out their candles and started a fire.

Which had kept him busy for all of about ten minutes. Now, each howl of the wind was echoing inside his very empty chest, rattling around, making him ache.

No. It wasn't the wind that was making him ache.

She loved him. She loved both of them. And they'd asked the one question that could ruin everything between them. Fuck. *Fuck.*

One look over at Dec, who had grabbed a stack of their expense reports — and was reading them upside down — told Micah everything he needed to know about how his best friend was feeling.

A low whine from the kitchen startled Axel, who lifted his lazy head from the couch and perked one ear. Micah furrowed his brow and dragged his sorry ass up to the kitchen. His phone was ringing against the countertop, vibrating teeth-chatteringly hard. Still, relief soared through him when he saw who was calling.

"Lily." His shoulders sagged, the panic leaving him in an instant. From the corner of his eye, he could see Dec whip his head around to the conversation.

"It's Maddy." Her voice was very, very slow. "Lils left her phone here and I just dialed your number from it to let her know. Why on earth would she be calling you?"

"Because she's forgiven us and wants to talk," Micah replied, before all of Maddy's words had set in. "Wait, you're calling here because Lily left her phone with you? When?"

"At dinner..." Maddy sounded the kind of confused that wasn't sure if it should be panicking. "Micah, what the hell is going on?"

"Is Lily with you right now?" he asked, though he damn well knew the answer to the question. "Madison, did she ever get down to the ranch?" Dec was up and off the couch now and Rosie and Axel were one step behind him. They knew that tone of voice better than anyone and they stood over by the door, waiting, watching patiently. Micah only wished he could be so patient.

"No, she didn't get down to the ranch," Maddy said. "She left with you guys — why on earth would she have come back with a storm on the way?"

"We got into a fight," Micah managed, somehow forcing the words past the tangle in his throat. Because fuck, *fuck.*

"She's not with you right now?"

"No," he repeated. "We thought she was with you."

"Jesus fuck." Maddy's voice caught, too, and he could hear the commotion of Ryder and Christian in the background.

"We're going out after her," Micah said. He smashed the speakerphone button and grabbed his raincoat and hiking boots as fast as he could. "I'm going to take the phone, but there's a good chance service will be out soon. We're going to get her back, Maddy. I swear to God, if it's the last fucking thing we do, we're going to get her back."

The same conviction in his heart was all too apparent in Dec's eyes, filled with dry fear that meant they had come to the same conclusion at the same time — they had just both made the biggest fucking mistake of their lives.

"I trust you," Maddy said. "Call me first thing. And God damn it, be safe. Because she's going to want you in full working order to kick your asses."

Micah's heart paused, frozen in that space of the moment. "She said she loved us, Maddy." He scoffed, the sound so incredibly soft against the roar of the storm. "How on earth can that possibly be true?"

He could almost see her rolling her eyes on the other end of the phone. "Why don't you go find Lily and ask her yourself?" she asked. Then the call went out, plunging their reality back into saturated focus.

"We pushed her away," Dec said, zipping up his windbreaker and testing the flashlight in his hand. "We fucking did this, Micah. If anything happens to her…"

"Nothing is going to happen to her." He zipped his own jacket tight, grabbed his emergency search pack and hoisted it high on his shoulders. Then he pushed opened the back door, ushering Dec and the dogs out in the fray.

It was even worse outside than he'd realized. The rain came down in hard, relentless pellets, a deluge that beat at his head and exposed hands. They couldn't take the horses or ATVs out in this. It would be too dangerous on the hill, even for the treaded tires, and the likelihood of one of the animals spooking at the many slashes of lightning cutting across the sky was too high to risk. He did take a moment to leash Axel, though, and Dec did the same with Rosie. While both of the dogs were more than capable of being off leash, especially in search and rescues, the leashes might just save their lives on a nasty fall too close to the edge of a hill, which was all too possible right now.

For people, too.

Fuck, *no*. He wouldn't even stop to consider the idea of her getting so much as a scratch on that beautiful freckled skin. He pushed ahead, stepping out of the relative canopy of trees and cabin overhang and into the storm. Dec was on his heels and they moved back in the direction they had come up from Triple Diamond, riding on hope. Most of the signs he knew for following trails, torn bushes, kicked-up dirt, something so much as footprints, were well and far gone with the rush of the rain, and the scents were so stirred up in the crash of water and wind that even if the dogs miraculously picked up a lead, there was no telling where it might actually take them.

For a while, they didn't try to speak. Micah had no sense of time passing, since the light didn't change and the storm never let up. The sky came in and out of brightness, thick cracks of lightning breaking through the curtain of smoke-like clouds and each roll of thunder could have very well been his heart bursting apart in his chest.

She loved him. And he'd let her turn around and ride away, into an oncoming storm, without telling her the truth.

He loved her, too.

At that moment, like a fucking miracle, another strike of lightning cut across the sky and Micah saw two things in the same instant. Cee Cee ran free through a clearing of trees, skittish in the storm and racing too fast to catch. The horse knew the way home, though, and if she wasn't back by morning, they could go looking for her. But the second, far more important piece of information was where they were. The Hut. The same little patch of mountain where he and Dec had…they had *made love* to her, here, not too many hours ago.

The sky glowed and crackled and he saw her the same moment Dec did, the same moment that a branch high above the Hut, where Lily was huddling against the storm, began to crack.

Everything slowed to impossible movement. He could see each individual raindrop in that moment, each ripe splinter of wood that peeled away from the tree, the frozen, terrified look in Lily's eyes as she saw them without really seeing them.

But she must have heard the crack, because she glanced up. She rolled off the porch, onto her side, then dragging herself the last few feet she could manage. The tree came down in slow motion, and Micah was paralyzed, frozen to his spot as the whole thing careened into the building, smashing the roof to bits. Shards of tree and house went flying in a thousand directions and the sound crackled through the forest as loud as thunder.

At first, he couldn't see Lily then he and Dec were taking off, the dogs hot at their heels as everything came back into real time, too fast time, too fast for his pounding heart, as he came around the uprooted tree to find Lily.

Or, rather, to see her. She was ten feet below the edge of the cliff, hanging onto the lip of the mountain with every ounce of strength she had. Against the wild beat of the rain and the slanting, pounding wind, she wouldn't be able to withstand much more and the drop below was into the sheer, pulsing, rioting darkness of the valley.

"Lily, hold on!" Micah shouted. He had the backpack off and was yanking the climbing cord free in the same seconds it took him to yell. "I'm going down there," he said, shouting again to be heard over the din of the storm. Dec nodded.

"Do you want me to go?" he asked, knowing Micah's weakness, knowing his never-leaving fear of heights.

Micah shook his head. "I'll bring her back to us," he said. "I promise." He yanked on the cord, still shouting as he tightened it around himself. "And when I do, I'm not going to make her choose." His voice was raw, but he carried on, actions and words pushing against the storm. "I don't care if you're by my side on this or not, but I'm going to fight for that woman and I'm going to do my damnedest to keep her."

Because Lily had allowed him to believe that he deserved happiness, that the choices he had made, when he chose to leave his home and many parts of his culture behind, weren't going to damn him for the rest of his days. She had convinced him, made him understand, somehow, some way, that he deserved love. And, God, he'd gotten hers.

"We can't let her go." It was ten thousand times more complicated than that, but Dec heard everything Micah wasn't saying.

"Together?" he shouted, his face sloshing in rivers of rainwater as he helped Micah latch the climbing cord to a tree. A slash of lightning burst against the sky, strengthening his resolve.

"There are way worse things than sharing the love of my life with you," he said. "Now, let's go get her back."

Then he was turning down the mountain in deliberate slowness, one foot, next foot, until he was able to reach her. Her eyes held panicked relief and her fingers slipped in the intensifying rain.

"I love you!" she shouted, her voice getting caught on the wind. "I love you both. Tell Dec, please."

"You tell him yourself," Micah said. He reached for her hand and her fingers began to slide off the mountain ledge. Stretching, pulling at the cord then...fucking bliss, he caught hold of her wrist and gently, slowly began pulling her up from the now cracking ledge. The storm surged and Micah let go of the cord in the moment to pull Lily close to his body. They didn't say a word, and Micah simply tugged on the rope, as he held Lily as tight as he could. They walked slowly, until Dec's head appeared over the lip of the mountain.

But just when Dec came into sight, a burst of light shattered the air around their heads blasting blinding light, sending a tree near the mountain's edge crashing to the ground. It tilted and swayed before pulling free of the earthen hold and plunging into the darkness, but not before smashing the edge of the mountain just a foot from where they stood, smacking against the rope holding them to the earth. The motion rocked Micah's body and Lily screamed, her grip on him loosening, fear knotting within him as he held tight against the shaking mountain, the ground and wind and rain pulling her from him in every direction.

The climbing cable began to fray where the tree had hit and Micah hoisted Lily high, pushing her up toward the lip of the mountain, trying to steady himself against the panic rioting in his entire body. The rope was going to fray and they were going to die, to fall to the depths of the valley below. It zinged, the pinging sound of a thread breaking. Then another. Then another. He tried to push Lily to safety, but she clung tight to him as they continued each slow, agonizing step together. Then he watched in horror as the last of the cable withered and thinned and, in frozen motion, unraveled against the night.

He fell.

Three inches, before Lily's small hand caught him around the wrist and Micah opened the eyes he hadn't realized were shut to see that Dec held her other hand, carefully maneuvering them back to the mountain's surface. Her hand was cramping and too small to get a good grip, but she held on with all of her ever-loving might and he could see every bit of her strength and power, as Dec dragged them, pushing through to get them each hard-won inch up the mountain.

"Lily," Micah shouted, desperate for her to know, to hear, in case they didn't make it to land.

She shook her head. "You have to survive so you can tell me," she shouted back. Then Micah heard Dec heaving Lily up. Her fingers slipped against his wrist, but this time it was Dec who grabbed hold, hauling all three of them backward and onto the muddy, wonderful, spectacular ground in a heap of sopping limbs. Not that he gave a fuck. They'd done it. They'd saved her. Together.

"I sprained my ankle," Lily explained, eyes filled with unshed tears. Because Lily Hollis was a fucking fighter and she would do whatever it took to see things through. Now that she was safe, though, and he was going to work damn hard to make her believe she was safe in his arms, she was allowed to lose a little of her staunch resolve and give over to the emotion of the night. "I couldn't walk and I realized I'd left my phone back at the house and… Fuck." She looked first to him then to Dec, her eyes bright with sorrow and regret. "I shouldn't have run away like that. I should have listened to you and talked things through."

"You have every right to be angry," Micah replied. "We gave you an impossible choice and it wasn't fair. We shouldn't have asked that of you."

"Well, it's not exactly fair for me to ask you to both be okay dating the same woman," she replied. "Assuming that's even still on the table."

"What are your thoughts on us loving the same woman?" Dec shouted.

Lily froze and he pulled her closer to his body, aware of the shivering and racking of her arms and chest.

"What did you say?" she asked, teeth chattering.

"We love you, Lily," Micah replied and, goddamn, his chest really did feel warm and glowing as he said it. "Fuck, I think I fell in love with you the day you walked through our door. You made me believe I even deserved a shot at love, made me realize how fucking incredibly, miraculously lucky I am to know you. So, yeah, I love you."

A sob caught in her throat and she glanced over at Dec. He shot her his trademark grin, only it was all real and no charm this time and, in that moment, Micah knew he could do it. He could love Lily and be okay with Dec loving her, too. Because he understood what it was like to fall under Lily Hollis' spell and another person who loved her as much as he did was all right in his book. It didn't hurt that there wasn't another man in the world he trusted more than Dec.

"Honey, you turned my life upside down in a hot second," he said. "Micah said it, but it bears repeating — you walked through our door and changed everything. Forever. So, for the love of God, say you'll stay and love us and let us love you."

She cried then and Micah released her so Dec could wrap her tight to his chest. With an uncharacteristic gentleness, Dec picked her up and the whole lot of them began the slow descent back down the mountain toward the cabin. Miraculously, they made it home and, dogs and people alike, they spilled inside, dripping like drowned rats and laughing their asses off, between rain-soaked kisses. They stripped, right there in the mudroom, peeling off soaked windbreakers and socks and boots and jeans. Lily's ankle was swollen and painful and so she iced and elevated it, while they called Maddy to tell her the good news, or rather, some of the good news.

And when the lights finally went out with the storm and they all gave over to the madness of joy and lust and adrenaline at having lived, at having found each other in the great madness of life, Micah knew, without a doubt, that they had their own light in their lives now, and that Lily would always be the brightness to guide them back home in the storm.

Epilogue

"I never thought ranger uniforms were sexy before," Dec said, his appraisal of her outfit so outrageous that Lily had to laugh. The uniform wasn't sexy. It was bulky and square and the pants were too short for her, landing two awkward inches above the top of her hiking boots. But she didn't care. When she walked through the front door to her cabin, *her* cabin, on the first day of her new job, to a home filled with two incredible men who loved her, she felt sexy and happy and free from so much that had held her back. Daniel would have approved of her choices, of her leaving the business in Mia's capable hands, keeping only a percentage.

And he would have approved of the men, too. By the end of his life, his patience for judgment and disapproval of the way others lived their lives had been long gone, and he appreciated love for what it was in any form.

This form, with Micah on one side, kissing the slope of her neck, and Dec pressing his lips to her mouth, was without a doubt her favorite.

The door swung open behind her and Maddy walked through and into the kitchen with a smug grin, followed by Christian and Ryder, who were eyeing the other men with overprotective suspicion.

"You can't kill them. I need them for things," Lily said, stepping in front of the much taller, much broader men, as if anything about her would serve as protection.

"I do not want to hear about *things*," Maddy said, as she unpacked a large grocery bag of chips, cookies, dips and paper plates. Lily glanced over and realized that Ryder and Christian both had boxes of beer in their arms, too.

"Well, I didn't want to see *things*, but here we are." Lily kissed Maddy's cheek. "And are we having a party?"

"Hell, yes, we're having a party! Not every day you start a new job and move a thousand miles from home, oh, and get your master's research get accepted in the fucking *Smithsonian*."

Lily blushed, but before she could speak, there was another knock at the door and Georgie and Darla stood outside, Darla with a stack of bakery boxes and Georgie holding more beer and wearing a grin.

Then, just like the night they first arrived, they spilled out to the patio, drinking and dancing and making merry. It was simple like that, the way Wolf Creek just accepted her, accepted the way she lived and the way she loved. And, by God, she loved.

She walked over to the far end of the patio for a moment of peace and stared out over the edge of the

Black Reef Mountains. A new group of survivalists would be arriving soon and the chill in the air and stark landscape out beyond meant that winter was no longer distant but right upon them. Five weeks has passed since the night Micah and Dec had saved her in the storm, since the night they had all saved one another, and Lily had come and gone several times, clearing up things at home, finalizing the business sales. She had tried to convince their parents to make the great move to Wolf Creek, explaining that her relationship had ended up just as unorthodox as Maddy's, and their mother had said that the Montana men seemed as good a reason as any to go, but for now they were just fine to stay put.

But now, her flat was rented, the store was in Mia's capable-business-partner hands and Lily was here. For good. Strong arms wrapped around her back and a bearded chin brushed her neck.

"You're the talk of the town tonight," Micah whispered into her ear.

"I'd prefer you to be the talk of my bed every night," Dec added, chucking against her skin. "But I don't blame them. You're worth talking about."

She went to respond, but something cold brushed her cheek, and when she looked up, she realized that it was snowing. Her first snowfall in the mountains and her eyes lit up in excitement. She grabbed both of their hands and looked out across the valley, taking in the full, grand view of the Black Reef Mountains and Wolf Creek, Montana. Her new forever home.

"I love you, Wild Flower," Micah said, giving her hand a squeeze.

"I love you, Lils," Dec said into her other ear.

She pulled them both tight to her body and murmured the words in return. "I love you." The seasons were changing. Soon snow would coat the mountains white then, eventually, the spring thaw would bring new life. But no matter what challenges they faced, no matter what the world threw at them, Lily knew without a doubt that she and Dec and Micah could weather any storm, as long as they were together.

Want to see more from this author? Here's a taster for you to enjoy!

Triple Diamond: Most Wanted
Gemma Snow

Excerpt

"Quinn." Ev fisted his shirt. His seeking fingers slipped below the waistband of her panties and found the slick, wet heat there. It had been a long week for both of them, and the second they had made it somewhere more private than a conference room at the FBI headquarters for longer than a passing glance, they had ripped at each other's clothes and made it as far as the couch.

"So ready for me, baby," he murmured against her cheek, the brush of two-day-old stubble a potent, animalistic aphrodisiac that made Ev arch up and press into his fingers with desperate need.

"Damn it, yes," she ground out, wanting him to go faster, to do something, *anything* to alleviate the insane pressure building within her.

"Patience," he said, but the increased speed of his fingers deep in her body belied his control and Ev simply pulled him down for another blistering kiss, dragging his shirt free of his dress pants and fumbling to unbutton it while distracting her with those lingering, achingly slow strokes.

"I don't want to be patient," she said around his kiss, biting, licking, kissing, sucking wherever she was able to get her mouth. "I want you. Now."

Quinn chuckled, but the sound came out low and husky and she knew he was as close to the edge as she was, as desperate to take her as she was to be taken, and the knowledge of how much he wanted her sent a new, far more potent wave of arousal surging through her body. He slid his fingers free so he could stand to kick off his shoes and yank his pants and socks off in one fluid movement. Even in the soft light from an early dawn, his skin glowed, dark and golden, contrasting with light-blue briefs that did little to hide how much he wanted her. Those piercing green eyes, as much a gift from his one Irish ancestor as was his name, Quinn Langston, scanned hot and heavy across her whole body, perusing her one free breast and her spilled, mussed hair and swollen lips.

"I fucking love looking at you like this, Ev," he said, voice raw with honesty and rich with arousal. "I love seeing you all spread out and waiting for me." His words, or maybe the tone of his voice, sent a new tremor of lust down her spine, and she shifted to push her slacks from her thighs. Quinn beat her to it, coming down to his knees between her spread legs and pulling her pants free way too slowly. He tossed them to the side, then slid his hand up her leg, moving in torturous circles near, but not near enough, to her covered slit.

"For fuck's sake, Quinn." Forget formidable FBI agent — right now she sounded about as intimidating as a horny bunny rabbit. Quinn only grinned, a rare but totally killer smile bright across his devilish face.

"Just teaching you a lesson, baby," he managed, and before she could get a word in, he lowered his head to her pussy and lapped at her wet, silk-covered hole. Ev gripped the couch so hard her muscles screamed, but the pleasure washing over her, demanding she simply give in to the release, was too much, overwhelming and wild, and she knew she couldn't hold it at bay any longer.

"Come, Ev," he said, his mouth still so close to her pussy. "Come now, baby." And it was the tone of his voice that did it, bursting the dam of her pleasure until all she could do was ride the intense, ferocious wave, screaming his name as she did.

Quinn leaned on the back of the couch to bend down and kiss her, a smug grin on his face and rare laughter spilling from his mouth.

"Shh, banshee," he muttered around kisses. "You'll get Lucas all excited."

Right now, Ev wouldn't have been bothered if her director at the Bureau called her into work, let alone that her roommate was asleep down the hall. All she could think about was getting Quinn inside her. About five minutes ago.

"Now," she demanded, loving the humor in those green eyes, loving that she could be the one to make such a normally stalwart, serious man smile. "I mean it."

He repeated her words, mocking with gentle sarcasm, then he stripped himself of the white muscle tank he wore, exposing toned, powerful abs, dusted in a light strip of hair that led down to the waistband of his briefs. Quinn liked to tease her. He was not a man to cede control easily — not that she was all that good at it either — and he enjoyed pushing her to the breaking point. Ev wasn't going to deny that she liked being pushed. She sat back and simply indulged in the slow ease with which he slid his briefs down those dark, muscled thighs, exposing a thick, throbbing cock she couldn't seem to get enough of.

Then he was there, right there, sliding her panties down and away, then teasing her entrance and not slipping into her wet pussy like she so desperately needed him to do. He slid across her wetness and she rocked up to meet his touch, to somehow steal the connection he denied her.

"Say it," Quinn demanded, control wavering, need coloring his voice low and demanding. "Say it, Ev. Tell me what you need right now."

"Your cock inside me, goddammit." The words came out on a harsh breath. "I swear to *fuck...*"

In that moment, he pressed deep inside her, stretching her needy body, turning the word into an expletive of pleasure. He was big, long and thick and it took a moment for her body to accommodate his size, even after all the months of them catching each other on couches and beds, ships passing in the night. But she did adjust, then she rocked into him with abject desperation. Quinn clearly wanted to say something snarky, but his control was more than fraying now. It was cracking right through and Ev knew she had him exactly where she wanted him—buried balls-deep inside her.

Powerful, controlled, all-important Special Agent Quinn Langston was at her mercy, and damn if that wasn't some heady shit. Of course, in a thousand different ways she was at his mercy too, but the only one that mattered right now was the way he drove potent, impossible pleasure into her body with every stroke of his cock. Ev wrapped her legs around his waist, pulled him as close to her as she could and rode him as wildly and desperately as he rode her.

She was so close, so very near the edge of breaking, that when Quinn brought his hand to her breast, the movement rough and needy, and stroked her nipple, she fell out from under herself, giving in to the ride, thrusting against him once, twice and once more before she shattered around his cock. The pulsing tightness of her pussy brought Quinn right over the edge with her, and he let out a string of curses and released inside her, thick and hot and enough to chase aftershocks of pleasure through her body.

He leaned against the back of the couch, catching his breath while keeping his weight off her, then bent down to give her a kiss. His mouth tasted like her desire, another reminder of this insane, combustible thing between them that had been going on for so long before either of them had realized it.

"I'll get us a towel," he murmured into her hair. "Be right back." He was slow and careful when he pulled free from her body, and Ev missed the feeling of him instantly, her skin cold without his touch. It was odd, that. For so long, she'd been so accustomed to being alone, to having friends — close friends, too — but just a few months into this new thing with Quinn had her all sorts of topsy-turvy and thrown off her axis.

And it wasn't *just* that she cared for him. She did, deeply and recklessly, the kind of emotion that scared the ever-loving daylights out of her. But according to her sister Aurora, those kinds of feelings were the good scary and she could objectively see that. No, those emotions, the fear she might ruin her incredible friendship, the potential for heartbreak, for getting too close — those weren't what snuck up in the middle of the night and gave her doubts and insecurities about the future.

But she couldn't bring herself to think about the creepy shadow thoughts now, not in the early dawn, with streaks of pink and gold cutting through the blinds and giving the false impression it was warm outside. No, not in the much warmer afterglow of long-overdue lovemaking with her very hot boyfriend, thanks very much. There wasn't anything else to think about, not now and not ever.

Ah, but there is, isn't there? Because if there wasn't then why would you keep wondering if this is it?

But before she could flay herself for *that* ridiculous thought, Quinn came back into the living room. He kept his hair short these days. Back in their early weeks at Quantico, he'd gathered the near-blond afro into a ponytail at the base of his neck and even in those very first times they'd gotten to know each other, Ev had wondered how he would respond to having his hair pulled in the throes of passion like they had just shared. Of course, he looked too young with his hair like that, too much the volatile, angry veteran he'd once been. Now, five years later, Ev could sit back and appreciate how he'd aged like a fine wine, all beautiful cuts of shadow and lightness, high, strong cheekbones and full lips demanding to be sucked. Of course, he put out a scary-as-hell demeanor, but she knew what it took to bring a man like Quinn Langston to his knees.

Literally.

"You're looking like the cat that got the cream," he said with a grin just as smug. He joined her on the couch, wiping away the remnants of the morning's activities with a warm towel.

"More like the cat that got *to* cream," she said before she could stop herself. What would her coworkers say about her now? Quinn wasn't the only one who put on a hard-as-hell exterior when he went to work. Ev could not only be an unapproachable ice queen at the job, but she'd worked hard to perfect the look, just as Quinn and Lucas had both created personas for themselves from the early days, whether they knew it or not.

Quinn opened his mouth to respond, but her phone went off somewhere and Ev jumped up from the couch, only just realizing how cold the room was when the movement made cool air brush her nipples and goosebumps break out across her skin. She wrapped a blanket around her body and grabbed her pants, looking for the sound. Locating it in her pocket, she answered without looking at the name.

"Monteiro." *Do I really sound so out of breath?*

"Well, I certainly hope so, since I haven't heard any news of a wedding."

Relief made her shoulders sag and Ev settled into the couch, tucking herself under Quinn's arm. He tossed another blanket over her bare body and she snuggled closer to him.

"*Tudo bem, mãezinha?*" she greeted. "Why are you calling me this early? I thought Dad was working the night shift at the restaurant now."

"Night shift, *pah*." Her mother's energetic tone gave Ev the impression she'd been up for hours and had used as much control as was in her arsenal to wait until after the sun had risen to give her youngest daughter a call. "Evangeline, your father owns six of the most successful restaurants in the whole state and you call it a night shift." In truth, it was an old habit from when her father *had* worked the night shifts in other first-generation Portuguese restaurants when she was only a child, but Ev knew damn well why her mother insisted on pointing out the number and level of success of each of their businesses every time she called.

"I'm happy with my job, *mãezinha*," she said. "And Quinn and I are still dating, before you ask."

Her mother *humphed*. "Well, as long as you're not married. But I do want you to know — Estela Patrício, her son is coming to town next weekend…"

"No, *mamã*," Ev said, keeping her voice firm. It was the only effective method of communication. "I'm dating Quinn and I'm very happy about it. Now, is there something else? Because we have a plane to catch."

Her mama *tutted*, repeated the information about Estela Patrício's son, *a businessman*, gossiped about Ev's sisters, gushed about her brother then repeated the information about Estela Patrício's son one last time.

Ev glanced at the clock mounted above their useless fireplace.

"I've got to go now," she said, cutting through her mother's sentence. "We didn't land until three last night and I'm catching a flight in, like, an hour." More like four, but exaggeration was another tried and true technique where her *mamã* was concerned.

Finally, finally, her mother wished her safe travel, bade her visit — *not next weekend, mamã* — and hung up the phone.

Ev sighed and glanced up at Quinn. He grinned, the sated, amused grin she didn't see nearly enough of on his handsome face.

"Don't laugh at me," she muttered, but he reached out and tweaked one nipple at the same moment, which made her squeal and wiggle out of his embrace in a vain effort to protect herself.

"I'm not laughing," Quinn said, hovering over her on the couch like the sexiest predator she'd ever seen. After a moment, though, he settled against her, fatigue outlining his handsome features. It was absurd they were even still awake right now. Still, her flight *had* landed just as she told her mother, nearly three in the morning. Quinn had been there waiting for her, after a week of them playing phone tag and sneaking in and out of the apartment while the other was dead asleep. They'd barely made it through the front door without ripping each other's clothes off and now it was morning — not that *morning* counted for a whole hell of a lot in their line of work — and all three of them had a plane to catch in just a few hours.

"Quinn…" This wasn't the first time they'd had this conversation and it wouldn't be the last.

"I know, I know, it's not 'cause I'm a black guy from the city." His humor was hollow and tired, but tinged with amusement.

"You're from Cleveland," she pointed out. "And it's not." Just as it wasn't the first time they'd trodden this well-worn territory. "It's only because you're not Portuguese. She wouldn't like me dating Lucas, either. Hell, she wouldn't even be okay with Patrick."

Lucas Vallejo would have given her mother kittens, but Ev's very white, very Western European boss Patrick Wickham wouldn't have passed the test, either. Ev was the only one of her *mamã*'s children to not bring home a Portuguese man, excepting her brother, who brought home different women with alarming regularity, and dear old *Mamã* was persistent in her task to single-handedly populate the Ironbound with the next generation.

She rolled her eyes. Her mother's antiquated ideals were still a solid presence in Ev's life, despite her being an Ivy League graduate with a top job in the FBI and approaching the birthday that would put her decidedly on the other side of her mid-thirties. "*Mamã*, she's old-school. Still hasn't forgiven me for moving to DC."

Quinn knew the spiel. In the months since they'd first moved their friendship into something more, they'd circled this conversation a dozen times, but it never made it any easier. Quinn's race, Lucas' race, Ev's sex — it had brought them closer together during those months at Quantico, surrounded by the pretty-boy country Captain Americas and the New England Ivy graduates who could have passed for their ancestors from two hundred years earlier. Being of any race other than white, or any gender other than male, put one at a disadvantage — a disadvantage that had led to one of the strongest bonds of friendship Ev had ever known.

"I know, baby," he said. He planted a kiss on her forehead and stood from the couch, moving toward the kitchenette with a slowness that betrayed his exhaustion. The city had been on high alert for terrorist activity after a series of phone calls, and Quinn, Special Agent for a Counterterrorism Fly Team under Lydia Brandenwell, who reported direct to the Secretary of Defense, had been busy in a way most civilians would never understand.

But she knew, simply by watching the slight limp in his left leg, an injury from an IED blast eight years earlier that tired more easily when he was fatigued, and the way his shoulders folded just a little. The only signs that Quinn Langston was running on empty.

"When did we buy this milk?" He pulled a suspect-looking half-carton from the fridge and held it up for her inspection. Ev grimaced and stood.

"I think the answer is too long ago. There's evaporated in the cabinet." Which was why she was still living in this apartment, had been even before she and Quinn had given in to their long-standing desires a few months ago. Between the three of them, Lucas, Quinn and Ev used the apartment about as often as one person did. Case in point, on closer inspection the milk was definitely chunky.

"We'll get something at the airport," Quinn said, tossing the whole thing into the trash without dumping it down the sink. *Good, way too early in the morning for chunky milk.*

"We should probably head out soon. TSA and all." *Ha.* She hadn't been on a commercial airline in years. Then again, she hadn't been on vacation in years. Still, when it was her boss and former trainer at Quantico, not to speak of one of her best friends, getting married, she flew her ass to Montana whether she was dead on her feet or not.

"Using you as a pillow," she said. "I don't remember when I actually slept last." *Which is probably for the better, since when I do sleep, I keep dreaming of...*

He nudged her out of the reverie and she leaned up to kiss his cheek, just as he went in for the kill, grabbing her around the waist and lifting her up with deadly aimed tickling fingers. Yeah, she was exhausted, sleep-deprived and headed for a flight into the middle of nowhere, trying to take down bad guys who kept coming back bigger and badder than before. But things were okay—they were better than okay. With Quinn Langston by her side, Ev had everything she needed to live a damn happy life.

Almost.

Home of Erotic Romance

Sign up for our newsletter and find out about all our romance book releases, eBook sales and promotions, sneak peeks and FREE romance books!

About the Author

Gemma Snow loves high heat, high adventures and high expectations for her heroes! Her stories are set in the past and present, from the glittering streets of Paris to cowboy-rich Triple Diamond Ranch in Wolf Creek, Montana.

In her free time, she loves to travel, and spent several months living in a fourteenth-century castle in the Netherlands. When not exploring the world, she likes dreaming up stories, eating spicy food, driving fast cars and talking to strangers. She recently moved to Nashville with a cute redheaded cat and a cute redheaded boy.

Gemma loves to hear from readers. You can find her contact information, website details and author profile page at https://www.totallybound.com

www.ingramcontent.com/pod-product-compliance
Lightning Source LLC
Chambersburg PA
CBHW020940180626
46814CB00003B/874